Other Books by Marian J. A. Jackson

Diamond Head (A Miss Danforth Mystery)

The Sunken Treasure

A Miss Danforth Mystery

Marian J. A. Jackson

Walker & Company
New York

First published in the United States of America in 1994 by Walker
Publishing Company, Inc.

Published simultaneously in Canada by Thomas Allen & Son Canada,
Limited, Markham, Ontario

Library of Congress Cataloging-in-Publication Data
Jackson, Marian J. A.
The sunken treasure / Marian J. A. Jackson.
p.   cm. —(A Miss Danforth mystery)
ISBN 0-8027-3191-0
1. Danforth, Abigail (Fictitious character)—Fiction. 2. Women
detectives—Fiction. I. Title. II. Series: Jackson, Marian J. A.
Miss Danforth mystery.
PS3560.A228S8   1994
813'.54—dc20   94-2816
CIP

Printed in the United States of America
2 4 6 8 10 9 7 5 3 1

For Frank Bosco
Thank you
I love you

Acknowledgments

As always, a special thanks to the New York Public Library. Without free access to the treasures stored therein, this book could not have been written.

I am also immensely grateful to my agent, Elizabeth Backman, for all of her efforts on my behalf, and to my editor, Michael Seidman.

Cast of Characters
(In Order of Appearance)

Abigail Patience Danforth, the world's first female
    consulting detective
Maude Cunningham, Abigail's companion
Jacqueline Bordeaux, Abigail's personal maid
Kinkade, Abigail's major domo
Malcolm Tibault, Abigail's millionaire host aboard *The
    Seascape*
Ariadne Tibault, Malcolm Tibault's second wife
Peter Tibault, Malcolm Tibault's son
Ehrich Weiss, Houdini, the world's most famous escape
    artist and psychic
Mrs. Ehrich Weiss (Beatrice), Houdini's wife
Jeramy Singleton, hunter of sunken treasure
Winifred Dupree, Ariadne Tibault's cousin
Thomas Perkins, captain of *The Seascape*
Amos Pettigrew, M.D., ship's surgeon
Boris, Malcolm Tibault's valet
Emily, Ariadne Tibault's lady's maid
Carlotta, a stewardess
A Stowaway
Paid crew of more than thirty
    and officers

The Sunken Treasure

1

Houdini, bound in chains and submerged in water, could defy nature and hold his breath long enough to escape.

Not so an ordinary seaman. The unfortunate fellow had seen too much while laying in provisions aboard *The Seascape*, the Tibaults' luxury yacht. Those intent upon preserving their secret did not hesitate to silence him with a blow to the head and, binding his ankles with chains not unlike those used by the great escape artist, toss him overboard.

Submerged in the Caribbean, he regained consciousness. But he panicked. Feeling the weight upon his legs, he gasped for air.

The apparent drowning was deemed an accident—no reason to delay the yacht's departure from Colon, Panama, for her pleasure cruise to New Orleans. Malcolm Tibault had money enough to bribe the officials and compensate the dead man's family. The crew, fearful of losing as cushy a berth as could be found in 1900, were easily silenced, since speaking of it might attract worse luck at sea.

Therefore, as Miss Abigail Patience Danforth mounted the gangplank and daintily lifted the hem of her voluminous skirts to her instep to gain the pristine teak deck, she was blissfully unaware that anything untoward had happened. However, the young detective was far from feeling felicitous emotion. The morning had been difficult. Her horse had balked at boarding the train that was to transport them overland. Her manservant, already miffed at having to accompany Crosspatches rather than be of service to his mistress aboard the yacht—though what he could have done for her he could not have said—had all but threatened to leave her employ upon the spot. Her temper had flared at Kinkade's cheek, and she had been forced to keep it at bay while resorting to her feminine wiles, which she possessed in good measure but despised using.

And that was not the least of it. As she greeted her host, flawless manners masked her concern, but all the while she was commenting upon the majestic lines of his ship, and admiring its perfectly raked masts and proportioned funnels, she kept a weather eye on her companion, Maude, and the manner in which she greeted Tibault.

Maude's gaze was as adoring as she had feared it would be as that distinguished gentleman, dressed impeccably in his blue jacket and white flannels, replaced his cap at a jaunty angle. Worse still, ignoring Abigail's presence, Maude slipped her hand into the crook of his proffered arm, forcing Abigail to follow in their wake as they made their way to the forward deckhouse.

Upon reaching the companionway that led to the guests' staterooms, Tibault lingered a fraction longer than punctilio required before he relinquished Maude's hand and, turning to a waiting stewardess standing nearby in starched splendor, introduced her. Much to Abigail's relief, Tibault remained topside to greet Houdini and his other guests, who were apparently even later than they. It was Carlotta, stiff skirts arustle, who ushered them down the stairs along a thickly carpeted hallway to their luxuriously appointed double stateroom on the second deck.

Ah, but Maude was blissful, which was precisely the cause for Abigail's agitation. Never before had she seen her companion so radiant. Her color high, her smile, once rare, now blossomed at the slightest wherefore. The sparkle in her eyes bespoke a delightful secret. And while Maude had said not a word to betray what such a secret might be, having just witnessed the effect of their host's farewell kiss upon her fingertips, Abigail now knew the cause beyond doubt. Since the answer had not tested her powers of observation one whit, she feared that others would be able to read the signs as easily. Having personally foresworn all emotion to better devote her life to emulating the redoubtable Conan Doyle's fictional hero, Abigail was loath to see her friend fall prey to the most commonplace feelings of all. Aware that to hint of such matters to her chaperon would constitute an ironic reversal in roles, she was at an unaccustomed loss. Should she speak of her concern? Or no. If she did broach the subject, what to say? And, knowing herself to be deficient in tact, how to say it? Truth be told, Abigail was not a little surprised that someone as suspiciously close to her third decade as Maude, if she were not already well embarked upon it, could still care about romance.

Abigail concealed her impatience as Carlotta showed them how to turn on the modern electric lights and open the portholes. She demonstrated the intricacies of the intercom by ringing for Abigail's maid, Jacqueline, who, from the dresses laid out neatly upon the beds, had apparently already unpacked, stowed their gear, and retired to her quarters in that portion of the ship reserved for guests' servants.

Maude listened to their discourse with half an ear. Captivated by the singing of a canary in its ornate cage, she drew close to the tiny bars and, poking a gloved finger through, twittered her delight with their host's thoughtfulness.

Groaning inwardly at Maude's childlike display, Abigail felt more kinship with the imprisoned bird than audience for its song. Soon the ship would be surrounded by an expanse of water so vast that escape would be all but impossible. Quelling the unwelcome thought, she feigned gratitude as Carlotta hastened to reassure them that the songbird was for their amusement only. She would, of course, feed it and clean the cage. Proclaiming herself to be pleased to grant their every whim any time day or night—they need only ring—she bowed herself out.

No sooner had the door clicked shut behind her than Maude took off her duster and discarded it on the foot of the bed that held her change of clothes. Pulling off her gloves, she dropped them on top of the crumpled garment, and headed for the dressing table.

Abigail strolled to the portholes as if her only care were to admire the view. The day was exceedingly fair for December, the sun having dissolved the high morning clouds. Remarking upon the fine weather, she unbuttoned her duster as she cast a surreptitious glance at Maude.

Intent upon removing her hat to facilitate the requisite change in costume for lunch, Maude sat at the dressing table to extract the long pins, all the while humming tunelessly.

Casually strolling to the carved chair at the foot of the farthermost bed, Abigail deposited fan and reticule upon the chair seat. Shrugging out of her duster, she draped it over the back of the chair, then tugged at the fingertips of her gloves to loosen them for removal. Gazing toward the portholes as though eager to regain the deck, she cleared her throat unnecessarily, and took the plunge. "Do you not think you are being rather too familiar with our host, Miss Cunningham?"

Maude stopped humming and, hatpin in hand, turned in the chair to glare at Abigail. "Well listen to Mrs. Grundy, if you please," she exclaimed before returning her attention to the removal of her hat.

Even though it was now obvious that she had given offense, Abigail nonetheless felt compelled to pursue the topic since they were all to be confined together in a small space for the next three weeks with the ever-present specter of boredom looming were the company to prove dull-witted. While Abigail placed no faith in the devil, she did appreciate that too much idleness created a breeding ground for mischief. Dropping her gloves to fall where they might on the contents of the chair seat, she added, "The way you flirt with her husband, one would find Mrs. Tibault quite blameless were she to fall prey to jealousy."

With great care, Maude placed her hat upon the dressing

table before turning again to face the young detective. "And are you not the tiniest bit jealous?" she asked with arched brows and wry smile.

"I?" Completely flummoxed, Abigail placed an innocent hand to her breast. "Surely you jest," she said heatedly. "You of all people know all emotion repels me. Why—"

As Abigail spoke, Maude stood and pointed an accusing finger at the outraged girl. "One need but look at you!"

"At me?" Taken completely off guard by Maude's remark, Abigail was distracted from her purpose. "Just what is it you are trying to say?"

Maude raked her with a glance. "That you feign ignorance makes my point." As if she had explained herself fully, Maude turned her back on Abigail and, stooping so that she could see herself in the mirror, smoothed her hair.

Not to be fobbed off by so cryptic an answer, Abigail strode to the dressing table and, hands upon her hips, stood over her stooping companion. "What do you mean?" she demanded.

Maude straightened up. For an instant the two ladies were all but nose to nose, glaring at each other. "Can you not see yourself?" Maude asked with a sweeping gesture of her hands to indicate that Abigail should look at herself in the mirror. "There you are, pretty enough to sit for Mr. Gibson—"

"Fanny feathers!" References to her comeliness made Abigail impatient whatever the source, and she retreated to the portholes with a swiftness that set her skirts arustle.

Even as Abigail moved away, Maude continued. "As beautiful as you are, not one single gentleman pays you court!"

Hugging herself defensively, Abigail turned to face Maude. "You know perfectly well that it is by my choice that I have no suitors." Drawing herself tall, she lifted her chin defiantly. "There is no place in my life for romance."

"And so you offend all who would pursue you with your dictatorial demeanor."

"I am guilty as charged, Miss Cunningham," Abigail said

without a trace of remorse. "I cannot very well unravel a mystery without using deductive reasoning." Her eyes darkened with resolve, and her voice was firm. "If this offends the male gender, so be it."

It was on the tip of Maude's tongue to warn Abigail, again, that she risked becoming an old maid, when something about the girl's posture caught her eye, and she stared at Abigail as if seeing her for the first time. "How like your father you sound," she said pensively, recalling Mr. Danforth's imperious demeanor. "Without question, you have inherited your mother's beauty—may she rest in peace—but it is he you have most begun to resemble." Moving away from the dressing table, she indicated that Abigail should take the chair at the mirror to remove her hat.

Realizing that they would be late for luncheon and the festivities attending their departure if she did not hurry, Abigail obeyed Maude's unspoken command without protest. Maude's observation had not displeased her. As she sat herself at the mirror, she sighed heavily. "Why, oh why, is it so wicked for a girl to have a brain?" she asked, not expecting an answer.

Nor did Maude deign to give her one as she crossed over to the canary's cage. Most of her attention was on the bird as she said, "Even you must admit that your morbid thirst for adventure is unusual, and most unladylike."

"Now *you* sound like Father." Abigail yanked the last pin free. Maude's hat, while modest, took most of the room on the tiny table, and Abigail cast about for some place to leave hers, which was considerably larger. The box for it was nowhere to be seen, and there was nothing for it but to put it on the pillow of her bed, which she did as she said, "The fact that I desire to do something with my life besides be an ornament for some man's arm is the very reason you agreed to travel with me if I recall correctly."

"Hah!" Maude exclaimed, turning her attention to Abigail. "Little did I realize that you would carry it to such an extreme."

"Extreme?" Abigail was genuinely puzzled. "What extreme is that, pray tell?"

"It is one thing for you to foreswear romance, but it is quite another to deny me a harmless flirtation."

Abigail held Maude's gaze. "Jealousy is no harmless emotion, Miss Cunningham." Her tone brooked no disagreement. "It is a capital motive for murder."

Maude rolled her eyes heavenward and groaned. As she did so, she began to fumble with the buttons at the back of her dress.

"Scoff if you like!" Abigail exclaimed as she checked the watch pinned to her bosom. "Now where can Jacqueline be?" she asked, motioning for Maude to come near so that she could help with the buttons.

"But you cannot be serious, Miss Danforth," Maude said, drawing close and turning her back to Abigail. "Ariadne Tibault? That mouse—jealous?"

"You are openly flirting with her husband."

"Are you quite sure you are not just trying to stir up some difficulty so that you will have a mystery to solve when we sail?"

"Miss Cunningham!" In the past, the accusation might have held an infinitesimal grain of truth, but in this instance she was positive she was guiltless.

"Why can you not be content to relax for a change?" Maude asked impatiently. "The Great Houdini is sure to be grand fun. I hear tell he will be shackled hand and foot, nailed into a box that is wrapped in chains, and"— Maude paused dramatically— "dropped overboard." She shivered with anticipation.

"Tomfoolery!" Abigail exclaimed, unimpressed, the last button undone.

Maude whirled around to face her. "But he might drown," she exclaimed, her eyes wide.

"Not very likely," Abigail said with a disparaging shrug. "There is no doubt some trickery involved."

"How can you say that, Miss Danforth?"

"Because he is an illusionist, Miss Cunningham," Abigail exclaimed impatiently. "By that very definition his entire performance is based on deception."

"But he cannot be a mere phony," Maude said with some heat. "He is famous the world over." It was not unlike Abigail to occasionally make outrageous statements by way of getting her goat, and Maude wondered if she might now be trying to pay her back for her earlier remarks regarding her lack of suitors as she continued. "Why he can escape from a straitjacket while hanging upside down from a flagpole atop a high building."

Abigail threw back her head and laughed heartily.

Grasping her gown to her bosom, Maude stared at her, bewildered by her levity. "I fail to see what is so funny," she said, aggrieved and suspicious that Abigail mocked her.

Abigail's eyes were bright with merriment as she said, "Who in their right mind would willingly place himself in such a ridiculous position in the first place? And to what purpose?"

"Well, to escape from it, of course," Maude said, as if Abigail were dotty for missing the obvious. "It is really quite mysterious how he does it."

Abigail shook her head, her brow furrowed reprovingly. "It is a mistake to confound strangeness with mystery," she said, pleased with the opportunity to quote the creator of her idol.

"Must you reduce everything to that infant science of detection?" Maude asked, her voice sharp. "If you are not careful, my dear, the very single-mindedness of your dedication is likely to turn you into a crashing bore."

Abigail very nearly laughed outright again. Nothing Maude could have said could have been more calculated to sting than the accusation of being a bore. Like her fictional hero, she aspired to avoid boredom at all costs, and the thought that she might be the cause of same would be an insult beyond bearing. However, Abigail was aware that a good defense sometimes lay in mounting a better offense, and by the very seriousness of Maude's attack, she realized that she had probably disturbed her companion even more than she had realized by criticizing her coquettish behavior. "Perhaps you are right," she said, her tone dry and noncommittal. She could not resist adding, "I still say you are treading on dangerous ground dallying with our hostess's husband."

Maude dropped her morning costume on top of her duster. Picking up the fresh gown, a veritable confection in pale green, an unusual color for her since her clothes tended to be somber, she turned to face Abigail. "I daresay if Mrs. Tibault paid more attention to her husband, he would not seek me out."

Abigail shrugged and sighed, a sound heavy with the weight of resignation. What could she say? Conventional wisdom decreed it to be the wife's duty to keep her husband happy because there would be no reason for him to prefer other women to her, or drink to excess, or resort to physical violence unless she provoked him or somehow failed him. This view seemed inherently unfair to Abigail as it left no room for the possibility of the man's being at fault by virtue of having mistreated his wife in the first place, thus causing her to respond in kind. But having lost her mother at birth, she considered herself unschooled in such matters, and in no position to judge. Since no one on the outside could delve into the privacy of a marriage to discover who, indeed, was at fault, she supposed that the wife might as well be held accountable because her husband was the only one who could earn a living. And he controlled the money even if she had inherited a fortune, which made her quite dependent upon him and, consequently, his good humor. Since the husband's lot was such a burdensome one what with the grave responsibility of supporting a household no matter the number of offspring that God provided, Abigail assumed her quibble to be an aberrant one, much like her determination to do something interesting with her life besides devote it to

one man. Although she did not presume to question the
status quo, if pressed, notwithstanding her loyalty to Maude
and consequent desire to see her happy, Abigail's sympathy
rested with Mrs. Tibault even as she wondered what that
poor lady had done, or not done, to precipitate her husband's
roving eye.

One other, not inconsiderable, detail troubled her. She
knew it was certain to upset her companion were she to
mention it, but she could not consider herself a true friend
if she did not at least try to bring the issue into the open.
Wishing to have Maude's full attention when she did so,
Abigail waited until Maude had slipped her gown over her
head and was smoothing it into place before she broached
the subject, first clearing her throat in an effort to banish
the concern that momentarily constricted it. "What if you
fall in love with Mr. Tibault?" With a piercing glance at
Maude's face to observe her response, she added, "He is not
free to marry you."

Before Maude could reply, there was an almost inaudible
knock at the door, and without so much as a by-your-leave
from either lady, the door burst open, and the diminutive
Jacqueline breezed in, apron strings flying.

"Oh, Miss Danforth!" she exclaimed breathlessly, shat-
tering every dictum of proper deportment by entering before
receiving permission to do so and speaking before being
spoken to. Hoping to forestall the scolding that was her due,
as she closed the door behind herself she continued rapidly,
"I apologize I am so long to come here. So many stairs! They
lose me." Before her mistress had time to reply, Jacqueline
spotted the hat on the bed. *"Mon Dieu, mademoiselle!"* she
cried. Horrified by the sight, she forgot herself entirely and,
turning her back on Abigail, dashed to the bed and snatched
the offending object from the pillow with an urgency that
bode ill for the delicate flowers that decorated it. "The
chapeau on the bed makes the bad luck!"

Distracted by her maid, had Abigail not been observing

Maude with a spyglass closeness, she might have missed her companion's answer to her question. Although she'd been privy to the sight for only an instant, the anguish that had flickered in Maude's eyes had been so profound that she feared the worst had already happened. In spite of her resolve to remain emotionally detached, her heart filled with dread.

▽

2

ARIADNE TIBAULT WAS no mouse.

Seated in the shadows provided by the roof of the after deckhouse, Abigail had a perfect vantage point from which to observe her hostess. With Maude sitting at her elbow, and listening to Mrs. Houdini's chatter attentively enough for two, she could not resist taking advantage of the opportunity to spy. However, the easterly wind that was proving strong enough to set sail by without the ship's twin screws, also destroyed the pretext of agitating the air for relief from the tropical heat. Thus, Abigail was forced to forgo the use of her fan. Given the strength of the breeze, unfurling that mobile curtain so indispensable for civilized discourse would draw unwanted attention, because the only remaining reason for its employment would be to catch the eye of, and carry on a wordless communication with, a nearby gentleman. And one such gentlemen, Peter Tibault, Malcolm's son, a clean-shaven, younger version of his handsome father, stood but a few paces away. He, along with his friend, the painfully thin Jeramy Singleton, was engaged in a lively conversation with Houdini, and Abigail had no desire to risk being mistaken for a flirt by any one of them. Of course the brim of her hat was deep enough to conceal the direction of her gaze from a distance, but the flowers that decorated the crown betrayed the direction she faced like a beacon. She was therefore careful to keep her head angled toward her engrossed companions so that the gentlemen would not catch her in the act of staring at her hostess, and think her rude.

Ariadne Tibault was tiny, her skin was Dresden fair, and the curls that escaped her wide-brimmed hat were blond. And given such a delicate complexion, had her eyes been pale, she might have deserved the sobriquet "mousy," but they were as blue as deep water. That Maude had been so far off the mark increased Abigail's unease. Maude must already be besotted beyond redemption if she felt it necessary to disparage her rival's striking beauty, or, worse still, was blind to it.

An awareness of her disloyalty for such thoughts did nothing to assuage Abigail's discomfort as she wondered anew why Malcolm Tibault would look at, much less dally with, someone as old as Maude when he had such a pretty young thing for a wife. Ariadne's offense must have been unforgivable. Even as she fumed at herself for acting the meddlesome old maid that Maude accused her of being, Abigail could not stop herself from wondering what the beautiful girl could have done.

Further, Ariadne Tibault was as gracious a hostess as Abigail had ever met, not an inconsiderable accolade as she had been entertained in some of the great houses of Europe and America. Abigail had little patience to spare for most of her sex who had nothing on their minds but clothes, who chattered aimlessly, and threatened to swoon at the first sign of difficulty. She admired spunk. Although Ariadne was exquisitely gowned as befitted her husband's station, the girl seemed to possess that quality in good measure.

As certain as sunrise, Ariadne had witnessed her husband's fawning behavior toward Maude when they had returned topside, and Abigail knew the dear girl's heart must have been bruised by the sight. But not by so much as a bat of lash or change of tone in her wispy voice had she given the slightest hint that she might have reason to be jealous of Maude. While introducing Mrs. Houdini, she had casually supplied that good lady with a conversational gambit, which had intrigued Maude, and set the two ladies talking as easily as best friends. To be clever and subtle with

introductions was a skill that Abigail had mastered only by
dint of much practice, and she was impressed to witness it
demonstrated so effortlessly by a contemporary under such
trying circumstances. Abigail was all the more impressed
when both Maude and Mrs. Houdini had responded to each
other eagerly, apparently oblivious to their hostess's tech-
nique.

Further still, as small as she was, it had taken but a
delicate flutter of her gloved fingertips for the musicians to
be persuaded to stop sawing away at Haydn and switch to a
lilting waltz. Although Abigail did not know its name, the
lovely melody sounded familiar, and she silently applauded
her hostess for her choice of music more suitable for the
launching of a pleasure cruise. She swiftly scanned the salon
to locate her host to see his reaction to the change, but he
was nowhere to be seen. Her gaze brushed past Houdini,
who was holding the gaunt Jeramy in thrall with an ani-
mated story, and she expected to find Peter Tibault thus
entertained. Therefore, it took her by surprise to see that his
attention was directed toward the musicians. A frown
creased his brow. Curious, she followed his gaze, but it was
not the music that was the object of his scowl. Rather, he
was glaring at his stepmother, and seemed poised to quit his
conversation altogether and stride over to her, presumably
to criticize her for changing the program. But just as he was
about to step away, Jeramy Singleton suddenly laughed
heartily and touched him on the arm. Startled, Peter took
the cue and, returning his attention to the two men, laughed
sincerely enough to persuade them that he had been listening attentively all along.

Abigail thought Peter's performance odd. What right had
he to question Ariadne if she changed the music? Sighing,
she regretfully pegged him as a stuffed shirt as he was also
a contemporary, a year or two older than they, at most. He
should have had no objections to, and by all rights, should
have preferred the modern melody. She wondered what
Ariadne would have done had he braced her in front of her

guests. Would she have burst into tears and fled? Like a mouse?

Then Ariadne spotted her cousin Winifred Dupree standing at the entrance and rushed over to welcome the unpleasant girl with a kiss. Abigail winced, and yet had to admire Ariadne's generosity of spirit once again. The effusive greeting was obviously intended to demonstrate to the assemblage that Winifred was to be absolved from any hint of rudeness for having been absent when the ship had weighed anchor. No doubt about it, Ariadne was doing her best to be mistress of *The Seascape*. No job for a mouse.

Schooner rigged, at 304 feet length over all, the yacht was not unlike a small city. To be sure, Ariadne had nothing to do with the actual running of the ship. That duty belonged to a well paid-captain, the charming, full-bearded Thomas Perkins, who commanded a crew of more than thirty able-bodied seamen and a full complement of officers. Naturally a purser and chefs were also in her husband's employ, but when it came to the crushing responsibility of planning the entertainment and menus, it fell to Ariadne to keep their guests and their palates amused. The reputation of the hospitality of *The Seascape* was in her hands. She was also, no doubt, responsible for balancing the guest list, and Abigail wondered whose idea it had been to invite Houdini. And though it was definitely none of her business, she also speculated upon what it had cost to lure him to come on board. Or for that matter, was he a guest? Was he going to perform at all? And, if so, for free? She was busy admonishing herself for such errant thoughts just as the great escape artist turned away from Peter and looked directly at her. A huge grin softened his naturally intense expression, and he winked.

Shocked and flustered, Abigail felt an unwelcome heat flood her cheeks. A rush of anger at Houdini for his unseemly boldness intensified her blush, and she felt reduced to a naive schoolgirl unable to control a show of emotion, utterly vulnerable without a fan to conceal it. How dare he flirt with her so outrageously, with his wife seated so near! Was the ship peopled entirely with philandering husbands?

Abruptly turning her head toward Maude so that her hat would conceal her flaming cheeks, Abigail's glance happened upon Mrs. Houdini's sweet smile and fluttering fingertips, and she instantly realized her mistake. Priding herself upon her powers of observation, misinterpreting the magician's gallant salute to his wife embarrassed her all the more, and she turned her gaze toward the sea to try to regain her composure.

Just as Abigail turned her back to Houdini's group, he broke away from Peter and the gaunt Mr. Singleton with a parting nod and, moving with a vigor more suited to the out-of-doors than the confined space the ship's salon afforded, joined their circle to stand by his wife.

Abigail was aware of his approach from his wife's greeting and introduction to Maude. Praying that her hat shaded her cooling cheeks sufficiently to pass muster, she turned to greet him and was immediately impressed with the difference between the Houdinis and their hosts.

Even when the distance between them was no more than the space one other person could occupy, the Tibaults appeared much like two strangers who did not care to become further acquainted. All of Malcolm's considerable charm seemed reserved for their guests. And Maude.

By contrast, although they had not been apart for more than a few minutes, and then not by a great distance, the Houdinis exchanged affectionate glances as if reuniting after a long absence.

Yet when Houdini turned his gaze toward Abigail, it was devoid of any flirtatious interest as he held one hand aloft to forestall an introduction. "Do not tell me," he cried, placing the fingers of his other hand upon his forehead in an exaggerated imitation of a spiritualist seeking information from the great beyond. "Aha!" he exclaimed, caught up in, and amused by, his own act. "You must be that daring young lady who aspires to emulate a famous character of fiction."

Abigail froze. Convinced that he had caught her misconstruing his gesture of endearment to his wife, she was equally sure he was ridiculing her. "I beg your pardon?" she replied coolly. She had shared none of Maude's enthusiasm for the magician before they met, and, having now met him in person, she actively disliked him.

Houdini closed his eyes as if seeking answers from far away as he intoned dramatically, "Is it not true you wish to emulate Sherlock Holmes?" Opening his eyes to watch her as she responded, his piercing gaze would have shaken a less confident girl.

Certain that he was teasing her, Abigail concealed her irritation with a gracious smile. "I assure you, kind sir," she said sweetly. "I have quite enough difficulty being myself to bother imitating anyone else."

"The great Houdini is never mistaken," he declared, undaunted, casting a knowing glance at Maude. Before Abigail could respond, Peter and Jeramy drew close. "And what are you so certain of this time, oh great one?" Jeramy asked. He was quite prepared to enjoy another joke, since the magician had just finished an amusing story concerning a mistaken identity. Knowing that Abigail had not heard it, yet wishing to include her in the fun, his smile was broad, and this time there was no mistaking the intended recipient of a conspiratorial wink.

Abigail blushed anew. Offended by the implied familiarity the thin man was taking with her she struggled to keep her temper in check. They had after all scarcely been introduced, and just because they were doomed to be in one another's company during the coming voyage gave him no right to assume liberties.

Houdini was oblivious to Abigail's difficulty. His full attention had been on his wife when he winked at her, and he had no idea that he had been observed by anyone else. Ignoring Peter's remark, he replied, "I do believe that Miss

Danforth and I might have a friend in common."

"Then you know Dr. Conan Doyle?" Abigail asked, her tone no more than politely civil, her composure barely restored.

"We have just begun a lively correspondence," he replied, surprised that the news did not seem to have the warming effect that liking the same author usually inspired in a new acquaintance.

Abigail looked at him askance. "I cannot believe that the good doctor told you of our tête-à-tête."

Houdini looked at her appraisingly. "I had no idea that you had actually met Dr. Conan Doyle," he replied, taken aback.

Bursting with curiosity, Maude could contain herself no longer. "Then how did you know Miss Danforth wishes to be a consulting detective?"

"I daresay he gazed into his crystal ball," Abigail said, her voice flat, as she glared at her companion.

"Nothing so ethereal, Miss Danforth," Houdini replied, intrigued by the lovely young lady's frosty demeanor. "The very charming Mrs. Tibault told me," he said, gesturing toward their hostess, who was engaged in a conversation with Winifred Dupree on the far side of the room.

"No magic in that," Abigail exclaimed, glaring at Maude in triumph.

Maude met Abigail's glare with one of her own. "At least Mr. Houdini is an honest man," she replied with a defiant tilt to her chin.

"I take it you do not approve of psychics, Miss Danforth?" The subject was dear to Houdini's heart. Sincerely interested in her answer, he leaned forward the better to hear her response.

Peter was about to make a clever remark when he noticed the serious turn the conversation had taken. With a swift glance at Jeramy, who also seemed to be eagerly awaiting Miss Danforth's answer, he decided to listen instead.

"Stuff and nonsense!" Abigail exclaimed with a dismissive wave of her hand.

"Ah, but Dr. Conan Doyle believes in them totally," Houdini replied. Wishing to test her sincerity, he continued. "He quite embarrasses me claiming that I have gifts. I would have thought that you would believe in spiritualism, too, since you admire his fiction so much."

"There is more than enough woe in this world," Abigail replied, her expression grim. As witness to the Tibaults' behavior toward one another, she believed it to be for the most part self-inflicted, but she kept that opinion to herself as she added, "I have no desire to contact another."

"Ah, but should you have a need, do you believe that you could communicate with another world?"

"To what purpose, I pray you?" She disliked being pressed for a definitive opinion by a stranger, in front of strangers, on so private a matter, considering her belief, or nonbelief, in a life in the hereafter to be her own affair. "Answers abound in this realm," she continued, deliberately sidestepping the issue. "One need only ask the right questions."

"But that presumes the person to whom you address your questions will tell the truth, does it not, Miss Danforth?" Houdini replied with a sly glance at their attentive audience.

"Hear! Hear!" Peter cried, exchanging nods of agreement with Jeramy and Maude.

Abigail bristled. "Well of course there is more to solving a crime than asking questions. Evidence must be gathered, clues examined, motives deduced."

"All well and good, my dear girl," Houdini responded, impressed with her cleverness and aplomb, his eyes alight. "But in your chosen profession, you are by nature embroiled in illusion."

"I do not agree, sir. I rely entirely upon my powers of observation and deductive reasoning, not mumbo jumbo."

"It is not your powers of observation that I refer to, Miss Danforth. It is the culprit who dazzles you."

Abigail had heard enough. "And you, sir?" No longer caring

a fig if she insulted him, she added, "Do you not deliberately deceive those who believe you have magic powers?"

"Alas, people want to be deceived, Miss Danforth," Houdini said gravely. Turning to his wife, he patted her arm as he continued, "Is that not true, my pet?"

Mrs. Houdini nodded in agreement, yet thinking her husband had gone far enough, she said plaintively, "Are you going to give away all of our secrets?"

Abigail was outraged. "And you take advantage?" she asked, scarcely able to believe her ears.

"I freely admit that I am an illusionist, Miss Danforth," the magician replied calmly, not in the least perturbed by the accusation in her tone. "When my wife and I performed as mediums, we deliberately created illusions. There was never any real mystery. Only that which was accorded to us by the audiences who wished to be mystified."

"But that is criminal," Abigail exclaimed.

Houdini shrugged nonchalantly. "That is show business—"

"Admit it, Miss Danforth," Maude interrupted. "The Houdinis are right. Not one of your adventures has ended up the way you expected it to."

Although quiet until now, Jeramy had been following the discussion with great interest. Before Abigail had a chance to respond to her companion's remark, he broke in. "I, too, must agree with them, Miss Danforth," he said in his kindly fashion. "Perhaps you do not know, but I hunt for buried treasure. It is not the actual gold doubloons and snuff boxes I seek, it is the idea that I will find—how shall I say?—untold treasure. Treasure beyond imagining."

"Hah!" Peter scoffed. "I will wager if you find any gold bullion you will change your tune soon enough."

"I daresay you're right, old boy," Jeramy replied good-naturedly. "But in the meantime, it is my dreams—my illusions of grandeur if you will—that keep me searching."

"Quite so!" Houdini exclaimed. Turning to Abigail, he continued intently. "When confronted with a mystery to solve, is it not your task to penetrate the deliberate lies and evasions of the culprit as you seek the truth?"

Again, Abigail had no chance to respond. So intent had she been upon the conversation, she had not noticed Ariadne's approach, and was startled when her hostess appeared at her elbow with Winifred in tow. "How serious everyone looks," Ariadne exclaimed in her feather-light voice. "Come, come," she said with a winning smile. "I'll not have any sourpusses on my ship." She waved her hands about as if breaking up a group of naughty schoolchildren. "It is almost time to dress for dinner."

Only too pleased to escape, as was Maude the moment Ariadne appeared, Abigail and her companion stood to bid their parting pleasantries. Including Winifred in their party, they headed straightaway for their rooms.

Thoroughly engaged by the magician and his wife, Jeramy tagged along with the Houdinis as they made their way after.

No one noticed, least of all Abigail who was already halfway down the companionway, that, except for the musicians who were still playing and a steward who had begun clearing the tables, Ariadne and Peter were left alone in the salon.

Having deliberately hung back in the hopes of creating an opportunity to speak with her privately, Peter blocked Ariadne's escape route to the door. Leaning close to whisper in her ear so that there was no chance for the steward to overhear, his voice was deep as a growl as he said, "How dare you?"

Ariadne pulled away. "How dare I what, pray tell?" She glared up at him, the expression in her eyes unfathomable.

"How dare you torment me so?"

"I?" Her smile was wicked. "Torment you?"

"You know perfectly well what I mean," he whispered, his voice hoarse.

"I do?"

"That waltz!"

She shrugged. "I can have the musicians play what I like."

"But that was our waltz."

She turned to leave. "He must not see us together." Before Peter could take her hand to stop her, she was gone.

As Peter turned and waved impatiently at the musicians to get them to stop playing, the pain was almost more than he could bear.

▽

3

MALCOLM TIBAULT WAS a simple man. And easily bored. Dressing for dinner was his favorite time of day, and, although he made much of chaffing under the meticulous ministrations of his valet, Boris, he enjoyed a careful toilette the way some men relished cleaning and polishing their guns. Or readying their paraphernalia for fishing. With nondescript family connections, his prospects as a youth had been dim for he'd been without ambition and had no desire for schooling. But he could charm a bird out of a tree. Possessed of a manly physique, a rakish smile, and heavy-lidded eyes that seemed to know a young girl's innermost secrets without her having to confess, it had taken no great effort on his part to capture the heart of the naive young heiress, Annabelle Simms.

Annabelle's father refused Malcolm her hand, but she was not only enraptured, she also was with child. Desperate, she disobeyed her father for the first time in her life, and eloped with her handsome seducer. Rather than see his only child, and grandson, live in poverty, Mr. Simms relented as Malcolm prayed he would, and relinquished the generous dowry due her from her dead mother.

Their marriage was less than tranquil, but when caught and forced to lie Malcolm kept his wife ensnared for the rest of her life with promises to change his philandering ways. Her considerable fortune, which he of course controlled, increased with her father's passing until by the time Annabelle died, there was nothing that Malcolm wanted that he did not already have. With one exception.

Pneumonia mercifully carried Annabelle away this Christmas past. Her heart had been broken long before her health, and had her lungs not filled with fluid, the scourge of syphilis might have taken years to painfully rot its way to a vital organ and thereby end her suffering. Malcolm's case was arrested. Shortly after his diagnosis by Dr. Amos Pettigrew, he was fortunate enough to contract a severe case of influenza, and with it a dangerously high fever, which had the mysterious side effect of putting the venereal disease in remission. He nonetheless suffered the precaution of yearly, painful injections of mercury and, paying Dr. Pettigrew a large sum to keep his secret, he succeeded in persuading the doctor to sell his practice to accompany him on his incessant travels. By nature restless, Malcolm relished his quasi-duty of overseeing his father-in-law's large estates in Hawaii, Panama, and Cuba. He and his wife, when she could be persuaded to accompany him, were entertained lavishly. Thus occupied, Malcolm did not interfere with the competent overseers. The doctor had seen little of the world, and he at length accepted the bribe, agreeing to also serve as ship's doctor when *The Seascape* was pressed into service.

Annabelle's disease quietly smoldered in her cervix for two years, symptomless, until a sudden onslaught of terrible headaches compelled her to call on Dr. Pettigrew in search of relief. Even as the doctor performed the usual leachings and prescribed draughts of morphine, both he and Malcolm knew the true cause of her distress. Having anticipated her visit, Malcolm paid the doctor handsomely not to tell her the truth. Thus Annabelle died unaware of her husband's final betrayal.

Nor was Peter told. Blaming his son for trapping him into the bonds of matrimony, Malcolm abdicated from fatherhood. Sudden access to wealth and the freedom it afforded blinded him to the very real possibility that without his wife's prenuptial pregnancy, she might not have had the courage to stand against her father's wishes. Malcolm felt he deserved her money—nay, *earned* it—by giving Annabelle his name and making her an honest woman. Peter was raised by a succession of nannies and governesses, who, truth be told, piqued Malcolm's interest and received more of his attention than their charge. Hitherto a devoted mother, even Annabelle was relieved when their son reached a proper age to send to boarding schools, and had not the temerity to desire another child. Therefore, when at nineteen Peter returned with the lovely Ariadne to introduce her as his prospective bride, only to have the visit turn into a deathbed farewell to his mother, he was a stranger. Even with all that transpired this past year, he was a stranger still. That he, quite possibly, might be an enemy never occurred to Malcolm. Trusting entirely in the power of money, he did not trouble himself with such speculations. Peter would be no better off than a pauper until his twenty-first birthday two years hence. And if he did not toe the mark, he would remain thus even beyond. Having a stranglehold on his son with purse strings, Malcolm did not trouble himself to consider Peter's feelings.

Nor did he consider the feelings of any other person who crossed his path, least of all the women he bedded. He cared not a candle's worth whether they loved him, it was the quest for the next one that kept him enthralled. He thought he had found her in Ariadne when she refused his importunings until he offered marriage. But on their brief newfangled custom called a honeymoon, he had discovered her to be no different from the rest, and began his search anew. Fortunately for her, Ariadne did not natter at him the way Annabelle had. Not being of an analytical bent, he did not realize that it was the search that was his quarry, not the conquest. Had he the wit to think it through, he might have realized that he was embarked upon an impossible quest. Even in the heat of the moment wherein he finally possessed the latest girl he had taken such trouble to seduce, he wondered what her successor was going to be like. It would have surprised Abigail no end to learn that Maude intrigued him mostly because of her age. He found that the older the spinster the more flattered she was and inclined to be grateful to receive any attention. Whereas Abigail did not appeal to him in the least. She had an unsettling, level gleam in her eye and an independent demeanor that he considered unbecoming in a female, especially in one so young. It bespoke an intelligence that he did not care to challenge. Until he had reduced her a peg or two.

"That is enough, Boris," he exclaimed testily. Even as he admired his white-tied perfection in the mirror, his tone said that this time he was serious. "I shall be late for dinner if you do not cease your infernal brushing."

Having trained himself to listen to the nuances in his employer's voice rather than his words, which for the most part he found empty, Boris immediately stopped his unnecessary whisking, and reached for the Jockey Club Eau de Cologne in the atomizer, which scent never failed to please. Mr. Tibault was usually full of gossip, especially when embarking upon a cruise with new people on board. This time, he was unusually quiet. Although Boris was curious about his employer's thoughts he knew, from bitter experience, not to inquire. Therefore, his face was a mask of noncommittal servitude as he spritzed the air around his perfectly groomed gentleman, and hastened to open the door.

Jacqueline fared no better. As usual, Abigail professed to care not a tittle for what she wore, yet she was critical of every selection Jacqueline suggested. Even though her mistress was truly beautiful when gowned and ready in raspberry silk with her mother's garnets at her throat, it seemed not to matter to her what she looked like.

To make matters worse, Jacqueline was pressed into service to tend to Maude as well. Normally, whether traveling upon trains or ships, or staying in hotels or private homes, Abigail and Maude had separate quarters, and this was the first time they shared a sleeping chamber. Nor had Maude ever before required the services of a lady's maid. This evening, not only had her mistress's companion sought her help but also by virtue of the shared quarters, she seemed to feel herself entitled. Jacqueline did not mind helping with an extra button or snap, or venturing an opinion on which jewels best became the neckline of a frock, but this evening's preparations were quite different, and she could but hope that it did not portend her duties for the entire voyage.

To be sure, there was a certain satisfaction in turning an ordinary, plain woman into, if not a public beauty, at least a younger-looking lady by dint of her skill with a crimping iron, some Parisian bangs that closely matched Maude's hair, and combs. The puzzle was that instead of being delighted with her companion's appearance, Abigail seemed actually jealous of the results, even to the point of ridiculing Maude in an attempt to persuade her to revert to her old-maid's hairstyle. But Maude was rightly pleased with her appearance, and in the green taffeta, which rustled daintily with her every step—another unusual addition since Maude rarely wore underslips that sounded the way they should—she was prettier than Jacqueline had ever seen her. Justifiably proud of her handiwork, her smile was genuine when she curtsied to their leave-taking.

But when the door closed behind them, and she surveyed the cluttered room she now must straighten, she sighed heavily and a frown creased her brow. The day had been particularly trying. Unpacking was easy enough, with ample storage space in the cabin and easy access to the extra luggage near her quarters. But getting acquainted with new surroundings and, most difficult of all, making herself understood in her halting English and nonexistent Spanish, was exhausting. Although she would never have admitted it out loud, she missed Kinkade. As much as they quarreled, Abigail's major domo was an invaluable helpmeet when it came to finding one's way about in new situations, and she could have used his assistance much more than her mistress's horse.

To perform her duties properly, she needed the cooperation of other servants. In a hotel such assistance was relatively easy to obtain because the duties of the various staff members were clear. Her mistress paid for them, so she was free to ask—and, if necessary, demand—help. It was much the same in first class on an oceangoing passenger ship.

Things were more complicated in a private household. Extra services were not paid for directly, and universally resented. An outsider needed talent for making friends easily. Depending entirely on the goodwill and sobriety of the housekeeper and cook, the servants of a guest could easily find themselves at the wrong table. Or hungry. Jacqueline's shaky command of English made her sensitive to imagined slights, and she found it difficult to cotton up to the resident laundresses and chambermaids, especially if they did not meet her demanding standards. And because it was a private yacht, *The Seascape* was proving to be the most difficult place to find her way about of all, complicated by how easy it was to get lost. One wrong turn and she was face to face with cheering, white-clad sailors who'd had the gall to poke each other and whistle at her before sending her off, red-faced, in the right direction.

Usually endowed with enough energy for two, she was weary as she ever so carefully made her way back to the cabin she shared with Mrs. Tibault's maid belowdeck. Notwithstanding the successful results, she felt it unfair that she be expected to wait upon anyone in addition to her mistress. Even Maude. Keeping Abigail's wardrobe in order in such a constricted space, however luxurious, was going to be trial enough. Yet it had not been lost on her that none of Abigail's grumbling was intended to dissuade Maude from using her services. If her mistress would not stick up for her, what could she do? To complain was to risk getting the sack. After all, she did enjoy dressing hair, and it was not as if Maude asked her to brush the hems of her dresses. Thus by the time she reached the door to her cabin, she had cooled her Gallic temper. Her day far from over, she looked forward to a nap instead of supper before she had to return and ready Abigail for bed.

But upon opening the door, her nostrils were assaulted by an unpleasant smell, albeit not an unfamiliar one on board a ship. She was about to turn away and search for a steward to clean up the mess that was surely lying about in the cabin, when she heard a moan.

"Emily?" Taking a deep breath through her mouth to avoid the smell, Jacqueline closed the door and, scanning the floor before she took each step, approached the bunk bed. Although it was supposed to be hers, Emily was huddled on the bottom. With some relief Jacqueline noted that the poor girl had apparently made it to the chamber pot.

"You are sick of the sea?" Jacqueline asked as she sat gingerly on the edge of the bunk.

"No!" Emily exclaimed, much too loudly. "I am fine," she insisted, though in a softer tone.

"But the throwing up," Jacqueline patted the girl's hand sympathetically, "is not all right." Gently, she placed her palm on Emily's forehead.

Emily twisted away.

Jacqueline frowned as she removed her hand. "How can I tell if you have the fever?"

"I am fine," Emily replied, her voice quivering in spite of her efforts to hold it firm. "I pray you, do not fret so."

"But something must be wrong."

"Perhaps you are right." Hidden from Jacqueline's view, a tear ran down Emily's cheek to the pillow. "I am seasick. I will be better tomorrow." Withdrawing a handkerchief from her apron pocket, she blew her nose.

Jacqueline could scarcely believe her own ears as she heard herself say, "Do you want me to help Mrs. Tibault get ready for bed tonight?"

Emily tried to lift herself to one elbow, but the effort it took was too much for her, and she fell back on the pillow. "Oh, Miss Bordeaux, would you?" she cried, holding her handkerchief to her nose to stem the tears of gratitude that threatened her composure in earnest. "How can I ever thank you enough."

Jacqueline smiled ruefully, and shrugged. As she stood, she was fairly certain that she'd be able to think of something that the girl would be able to do to return the favor, but at that moment she was just too tired to think what it might be.

Dinner had been superb, as anticipated, with splendid wines accompanying each course. Presumably their brandy and cigars had been equally satisfactory, and the gentlemen all seemed content as they joined the ladies in the second-deck salon. The paneled room creaked and groaned with the motion of the ship, much like a favorite rocking chair, but since the night air had turned a bit cool, Malcolm declared that it would be more comfortable to gather there for the evening's entertainment. Small by the standards of a drawing room in a house, it was exceptionally commodious for a ship, with built-in, overstuffed double settees separated by an ornate wooden armrest, which followed the graceful inside curve of the room, and enough matching overstuffed chairs and side tables holding after-dinner refreshments to accommodate the Tibaults and their nine guests. An upright piano with a collapsible stool dominated the wall by the door, and the chairs were arranged facing it, as if to hold an audience for a concert.

Even though it made her feel like an old-maid gooseberry, Abigail was nonetheless determined that Malcolm would not have a chance to sit beside Maude, and when Maude chose the inside settee, leaving the space beside her next to the armrest free, she ignored Maude's glare, and took it.

Ariadne scarcely looked up when her husband entered the room, and he, in turn, did not deign to look at his wife as he made himself comfortable in the chair next to Mrs. Houdini as Abigail had been inconsiderate enough to render Maude inaccessible.

Peter had no difficulty fitting himself next to Jeramy Singleton who took up little space on the remaining settees next to Abigail. Dr. Pettigrew and Captain Perkins waited until Winifred had changed chairs to be nearer the piano before taking the remaining two. Houdini remained standing by the piano. Maude leaned forward eagerly, and Abigail groaned inwardly, when he began to speak. The magician had no intention of playing the instrument, of course, it was simply the logical place to stand to begin his performance.

Even Abigail was impressed by his dexterity as he manipulated a deck of cards, and she had to remind herself that he himself had admitted it was trickery and deception he used, not real magic. By the time he ended the card tricks by having Ariadne discover her choice of the three of spades in the captain's vest, she was clapping in earnest.

Before the clapping died down, Malcolm suggested that Houdini give a demonstration of thought reading. Since everyone else clapped even harder with anticipation, not wishing to be a spoilsport, Abigail leaned back and unfurled her fan to hide her annoyance. But when she, along with everyone else, was handed a slip of paper and invited to write a message, she dutifully wrote, "Mr. Houdini is a clever gentleman, indeed" and, folding the note so that her script would not show, tossed it into a salad bowl that had been pressed into service.

Placing one of the side tables in front of the piano with the bowl of folded papers on top, Houdini sat on the piano stool, facing his audience. Pulling her chair close, his wife acted as his assistant. Waiting until the room was absolutely still, he closed his eyes and plunged his hand into the bowl to draw out a slip of paper. Placing the note on his forehead he paused dramatically before he said, "The sun shall rise in the east tomorrow morning." Opening his eyes, he glanced around expectantly as he handed his wife the note.

Abigail was about to howl with laughter at the obvious chicanery when Malcolm stood, his face ashen. "But that is exactly what I wrote," he cried. "How did you do that?"

The room burst into sound with applause. And so it went with all the messages.

Even as she was impressed by how banal most of the notes

were, Abigail became even more certain that there was a hoax involved, but she could not figure out how he did it.

Not so the rest of the audience, who believed him to be a genius. By the time he was done, all but she cheered with enthusiasm and wonderment. Much to her embarrassment, after a short bow to acknowledge the applause, the magician turned his piercing gaze directly toward her. "I see you are not impressed, Miss Danforth. Even though your note called me a clever fellow?"

"I do believe that there is some trickery afoot, sir," Abigail said with a defiant tilt to her chin.

"We have not met before this day, have we, Miss Danforth?"

Maude looked up at her expectantly. Ariadne and Winifred twisted in their chairs for a better view. Malcolm Tibault had his fingers to his lips, and looked for all the world like he was hiding a smile. She could not tell for certain what Jeramy and Peter's reactions were, but she could feel their expectant silence. Even the captain and doctor seemed intrigued. Unless she was to be forever branded as rude and unable to play her part as a guest, Abigail had no choice but to go along with the farce.

"No, sir." She summoned a smile from Miss Donner's class in deportment to conceal her fury at being put on the spot in front of strangers, by a stranger, and a charlatan at that. "We have not."

"May I have your permission to ask if some of the impressions I am receiving about you are true?"

Since it was utterly impossible for Abigail to reply otherwise, she gritted her teeth, managed an even larger smile, and nodded her assent.

Houdini strode to the far side of the piano. He stood silently for a moment. Not a breath stirred in the room. Suddenly he turned, and again looked directly at Abigail. "Did your mother die when you were born, Miss Danforth?"

"Yes, sir," Abigail looked around the room as she responded. "Anyone here could have told you that." Her smile was wicked as she continued, "Might I add that I have no desire to get in touch with her."

Winifred fanned herself vigorously to conceal a sudden fit
of the giggles, while the gentlemen made various coughing
sounds and settled themselves more comfortably in their
chairs.

Although certainly aware of the restlessness of his audience, Houdini was unperturbed. "And your father never
remarried," he continued, looking directly at her.

"Also common knowledge," Abigail replied coolly.

"And does everyone also know that you have twin brothers?"

Abigail turned to glare at Maude. "Miss Cunningham!"
she exclaimed.

Innocent, and heartily offended by the accusation, Maude
opened her mouth to protest, but before she could speak,
Houdini continued.

"I do believe that Benjamin is two minutes older than
Rodney?"

"How dare you discuss my family with . . . with strangers," Abigail cried, still glaring at Maude.

Again, before Maude could speak, Houdini continued.
"Correct me if I am wrong, but I do believe that you ride your
horse Crosspatches astride."

"I say!" Peter exclaimed.

"Does she now," Jeramy said, impressed.

To a man, the gentlemen expressed their astonishment at
such an uncommon practice, while the women stared at her
as if she were daft.

While the room was abuzz, Maude leaned close. "I swear
to you, Miss Danforth, I did not tell him anything," she said,
crossing her heart.

Although nothing the magician said had been detrimental
to her or her family, Abigail resented the intrusion on her
privacy. She gained her feet to better protest.

Instantly, the gentlemen all stood.

Even though she knew she was causing the entire party
discomfort, Abigail remained standing. "All that you have
said proves nothing!"

"You are quite correct, Miss Danforth," Houdini replied

with a glint of respect in his eye that was quite lost on Abigail. "But what if I told you that I know you have decided to never carry a gun again."

Abigail was stunned. She had made that decision alone in the dead of night in her quarters in the Humbolt's private varnish. It did not matter to her if the whole world knew, but she had not told another living soul.

There was no mistaking Abigail's reaction, and Houdini's audience was much impressed as she slowly sat down.

The men remained standing as they clapped.

In the innermost bowels of *The Seascape* where the racket of wood grating against wood was loudest, there was a hold where trunks of clothes, emergency sails, and boxes of unspoilable, unneeded supplies were stowed. An exceedingly clever person had stacked the boxes and trunks to create a crawl space that led to a cul-de-sac just large enough to shelter an average-sized man. Its exact whereabouts known only to its inhabitant, the cave was so cleverly hidden that anyone opening the hold, even had he held a light aloft and disturbed the top layer of boxes, could not find the entrance.

Because of the necessity of secrecy, he was doomed to be sparsely fed and underexercised. As short and swift as his passage promised to be, time passed slowly in the noisy dark, but not because of hunger and boredom. Those privations were nothing compared to the torment of his conscience as he contemplated the innocent seaman's death. Now there was no turning back. He had no choice but to endure the waiting. And not get caught.

$\triangledown$

4

"I SWEAR IT, Miss Danforth." Jacqueline stood stiff as any private facing his sergeant. Her right hand rested upon her heart, and her left reached toward heaven as a rod for lightning bolts if her words were not sooth. "On the heart of my sainted mama, I never speak to *Monsieur* or *Madame* Houdini."

"Come, come, Miss Danforth," Maude said, releasing the corner of the birdcage nightcloth. "This inquisition has gone on long enough. Can you not see the poor girl is telling the truth? You had best excuse her to tend Mrs. Tibault."

Jacqueline slowly lowered her hand and stared at Maude in astonishment.

"Miss Danforth and I can manage a few buttons between us." Offended by Jacqueline's surprised expression that implied that they might not be able to dress themselves for bed without her, Maude's tone was brisk. "I have always braided my own hair, and I daresay Miss Danforth can manage for one night." With a twinkle in her eye, she added, "If not, I shall enter the fray."

Scarcely able to believe her ears, and vastly relieved since Emily's moaning had robbed her of her nap, Jacqueline looked back at her mistress for permission.

"Very well, you may go." Abigail's temper had cooled, leaving her with a thousand questions. Before Jacqueline could get the door closed, she motioned for Maude to come close so that she could begin unhooking her companion's gown. "Well, Miss Cunningham?" she asked when Maude had complied.

"I warn you, Miss Danforth." Maude turned her head so that she could speak over her shoulder while Abigail busied herself with buttons and hooks. "I will not stand here and have you accuse me like one of your suspects."

"You did visit the Tibaults in Hawaii numerous times without me." Abigail kept her tone noncommittal as she busied herself with her nimble fingers. "Who knows what you might have let slip?" Pausing, she shrugged as she added, "In all innocence, of course."

Maude turned around to face Abigail, forcing her to stop. "Have you never considered that he just might be clairvoyant?"

"Fanny feathers!" Abigail exclaimed. Annoyed, knowing she was taking a liberty, she nonetheless placed her hands on Maude's hips and, forcefully turning her companion around, completed her task in silence, whereupon Maude returned the favor, also in silence.

Both were gowned for sleep. Seated in front of the mirror, Abigail had just placed the hairbrush on the dressing table after completing the hundredth stroke. Separating her waist-length hair into thirds she began deftly braiding it when Maude drew close.

Addressing Abigail's reflection in the mirror, Maude asked, "Have you truly forsworn the protection of a gun?"

Concentrating on braiding her hair, Abigail refused to meet Maude's gaze in the mirror. "I could not live with myself if I killed another human being," she replied.

"What about the culprits you bring to justice?" Leaving Abigail's side, Maude took the few steps to her bed and, shedding her dressing gown, draped it across the footboard. "Do they not face the death penalty for murder?" she asked as she climbed into bed.

"After a fair trial," Abigail said impatiently. Her braid complete, she stood to follow Maude's lead into bed. "It is not the same thing at all."

"I daresay your hair splitting does not hold much comfort for the poor wretch being hanged," Maude replied. Fussing

with the bedclothes she added, "Have you no thought for
your own safety?"

"London bobbies manage quite nicely without pistols,
why shouldn't I?" Abigail paused before adding with a shake
of her head, "How Houdini found out is a puzzlement."

"Why do you not ask him?"

"He found out about me without asking me directly,"
Abigail said, furrowing her brow thoughtfully. Pulling the
covers to her chin she continued with a sly smile. "Two can
play that game."

Jacqueline let herself out of Mrs. Tibault's stateroom, her
face a study in perplexity. She'd had but one mistress before
being rescued by Abigail and, blessings be, her employment
with that harridan had been brief. Her father, a Parisian
cobbler, might have made enough money to support his
family had it not included thirteen children. The second
oldest, and first girl, Jacqueline had vowed she'd never marry
and become a brood-mare like her mother. She'd been only
too happy to abandon her native tongue for English for the
opportunity to cast her lot with the beautiful, wealthy, and,
by comparison, even-tempered Abigail who apparently intended to travel a great deal, thus providing her with a
chance to see the world. Nothing in her subsequent experience had prepared her for these past two nights serving the
likes of Ariadne Tibault, and she desperately needed someone to talk to.

Emily was out of the question as a confidante since it was
Emily's job that Mrs. Tibault had as much as offered her if
the girl's health did not improve in a hurry. To tell Abigail
that her hostess was trying to steal her away was unthink-
able. Abigail just might get angry and tell her to be gone, and
good riddance. At the very least it would be sure to start a
quarrel, and no matter who won she would be the loser.
Never had she missed Kinkade more.

As she drew close to her quarters, even though she had
just finished readying Mrs. Tibault for bed and it was too

late for Emily's help, she crossed her fingers that the girl had begun to feel better and would not be in their cabin. The smell that greeted her as she opened the door dashed her hopes.

Lighting the whale-oil lamp mounted on the wall, she tiptoed to the bunk and, sitting on the edge, patted Emily's hand until she opened her eyes. "Mrs. Tibault orders you to see Dr. Pettigrew," she lied.

"I do not want a doctor," Emily whined, withdrawing her hand.

Jacqueline wearily gained her feet. Guilt and a large measure of disdain for the girl's lack of spirit, not to mention the burden of carrying her duties, combined to erase the sympathy she had initially felt at Emily's plight. It was not without satisfaction that she stared into the darkness where the girl lay moaning, and said, "She will give you the boot if you do not."

"I will be fine when we reach dry land," Emily replied, making her voice stronger to convince Jacqueline.

"Do you have the *mal de mer* always?" Jacqueline asked, surprised that Mrs. Tibault would bring her along if her affliction was known.

"There is a first time for everything," Emily replied in a vain attempt at levity. "You have been a brick, Miss Bordeaux." Her voice gained strength. "I do hope Miss Danforth is not getting peckish on my account."

"Miss Danforth is the saint, and Miss Cunningham another, but I am tired." Jacqueline sighed heavily as she reached for the pins in her cap. "When Carlotta brings the breakfast, why not ask her to take your place?"

"Would you ask an upstairs parlor maid to assume the duties of a lady's maid?" Emily replied haughtily.

Jacqueline had had enough, and her temper got the better of her. "If you do not see Dr. Pettigrew at first light, I . . . I . . . " She shook her finger at the shadows in the lower bunk, trying to think of something to blackmail Emily with. It did not occur to her that the girl was anything but a virgin, but having witnessed her own mother's similar symptoms often enough, and it being the worst thing she could think of to say, she continued, "I tell everybody you have the baby coming!"

Emily swooned dead away.

That she received no smarty reply merely convinced Jacqueline that she had made her point. Readying herself for bed in righteous silence, she climbed into the top bunk unaware that Emily had not merely fallen asleep.

The wind was brisk, thus there was no further need to stoke the noisy, soot-producing engines as *The Seascape* made way under sails taut with power. Strolling on the promenade deck with Mrs. Houdini, Abigail was grateful for the lead pellets that Jacqueline had sewn in her hems. Even thus weighted, she kept a cautious hand at the ready lest her skirts fly an indecorous inch and reveal a booted ankle. Her hat was held fast with French netting tied in a becoming bow under her chin, leaving two streamers of lace to float in her wake.

Much to Abigail's delight, Mrs. Houdini had proved to be not at all high-hatty as the wife of a famous man might justifiably be, and had cheerfully agreed that a brisk walk would do her good and, except for her husband of course, she could think of no more felicitous companion than Abigail. The graciousness with which she had accepted Abigail's invitation had surprised her, as she had all but insulted the woman's husband by accusing him of trickery on their first night out. Unless the lady was a simpleton, which Abigail doubted since even she had to concede that whatever else Houdini was, he was more intelligent than most and would not have tolerated a dullard for an assistant, his wife was no doubt smart enough to suspect that she had an ulterior motive. Loath to insult the woman's intelligence, the moment they were out of earshot of the others, Abigail said, "You have perhaps guessed why I have asked you to join me in a constitutional?"

"I confess I have an idea, Miss Danforth." Easily keeping

in step with Abigail, whose stride was just this side of ladylike, Mrs. Houdini continued. "But rather than have me guess, why do you not simply tell me?"

"Very well." Abigail drew a deep breath and plunged ahead before she lost her nerve. "Your husband's thought reading of the notes from the salad bowl was a trick, was it not?"

Mrs. Houdini's delighted smile as she glanced at Abigail was all the corroboration the young detective needed.

"But how—?"

"There is nothing mysterious about it, Miss Danforth. Would the knowledge that my husband always works with a confederate provide you with a clue?"

"Someone in addition to you?"

Mrs. Houdini nodded. Her expression encouraged Abigail to speculate further.

"Aha!" Abigail exclaimed, stopping in her tracks. "It was Mr. Tibault, I do believe."

"Exactly." Mrs. Houdini drew still beside her.

"And Mr. Houdini leaves Mr. Tibault's note for the last!" Abigail exclaimed, a triumphant gleam in her eye.

With a congratulatory nod, Mrs. Houdini resumed walking.

Abigail fell into step beside her. "Why, pray tell, are you so willing to reveal your husband's secrets to me?"

"My husband is not one to plume himself with false feathers, Miss Danforth," she replied, without slowing her pace. "He respects gumption in a girl, which you seem to possess in good measure. Furthermore, you both admire Dr. Conan Doyle."

"Then do you mind telling me where he got his information about me?"

"Not in the least." Mrs. Houdini cast a swift, penetrating glance at Abigail as she said, "From your Miss Bordeaux."

Again, Abigail stopped in her tracks, her face a cloud of disapproval. "Jacqueline lied to me?"

Mrs. Houdini paused long enough to turn and face Abigail. "Perhaps she did not realize what she was doing?" she said before resuming her brisk pace.

"How can that be?" Abigail exclaimed angrily, catching up to her. "She swore that she had not spoken to you."

"Ah, but it was Mrs. Tibault's Emily who talked to your lovely maid. Servants do love gossip, do they not? What better topic than their employers?"

"But Jacqueline knew nothing of my decision about guns. How did he—?"

"Alas, I do not have the answer to that one, my dear." She smiled as she added, "My husband is passing clever, even if what he does is all humbug and trickery. You must speak to him directly on that score."

Abigail did not wait for Maude to close the door to their stateroom behind her before she rang for Jacqueline, and began removing her gloves.

"I fail to see why you are so upset, Miss Danforth." Releasing the handle of the door, Maude walked over to the birdcage to greet the canary that had burst into song upon their arrival.

"It was not you who had their family paraded in front of strangers," Abigail exclaimed impatiently, untying the lace streamer that anchored her hat.

"I fail to see the harm—!"

"You fail to see a great deal, my friend—"

"I would ask you not to call me your friend in that tone of voice," Maude interrupted. "Irony does not become you."

Having placed her hat on the dressing table, Abigail seated herself on the edge of her bed and lifted her skirts to begin unlacing her boots. Before she could reply, there was a soft knock at the door, and Jacqueline entered. Abigail abandoned her laces along with her response to Maude to sit up straight and glare at her maid. "How dare you discuss my affairs with servants!" she said without preamble, shaking a disapproving finger at her before the hapless girl could get the door closed.

Not knowing what her mistress was talking about, Jacqueline stood in front of her and, clasping her hands in front of her apron, fearing that she was about to be let go, stared down at them.

"Speak up, girl." Leaving her spot by the birdcage, Maude reached for the pins in her hat as she moved toward the dressing table.

Abigail glared at Maude. "I will conduct this interview if you please, Miss Cunningham," she said in a tone that brooked no nonsense. Returning her attention to her maid, Abigail's frown was most forbidding.

Jacqueline looked up from her hands to gaze at Abigail earnestly, still not knowing what she had done to so anger her mistress that she would not allow her to begin readying her for dinner.

Abigail shook an angry finger at her maid. "Just exactly what did you tell Emily?"

"Miss?—" Jacqueline looked at Abigail blankly.

"Did you or did you not tell Mrs. Tibault's maid that my mother died and that I had twin brothers?"

"*Oui*, but—"

Abigail turned to stare at Maude triumphantly. "And Emily told Mrs. Tibault, who told Mrs. Houdini, who told her husband, who singled me out in front of the entire party on this ship to tell me."

As Abigail spoke, Jacqueline's eyes opened wider and wider, as did her mouth until by the time Abigail had finished speaking she was staring at her mistress in open-mouthed amazement.

As was Maude.

"So much for psychic ability," Abigail exclaimed.

"Well, I never," Maude said, sinking slowly to sit on the dressing table chair.

Jacqueline was distraught. "But I did not mean to—"

Ignoring her maid's response, Abigail stood and, turning her back to Jacqueline, gestured for her to commence with her duties. "I must insist that you stop telling the other servants my business."

Sensing that there was hope that the crisis had passed and that her position as lady's maid was saved, Jacqueline's fingers flew.

"Is there anything else you told this Emily person that I should know about?" Abigail asked.

"No, miss." Jacqueline stopped unbuttoning Abigail's gown long enough to cross herself.

"Why not ask her if Emily had anything to say about the Tibaults," Maude said.

"Miss Cunningham!" Abigail exclaimed, horrified. On second thought, she turned to face Jacqueline. "Well?" she asked.

"Miss?" Jacqueline gazed up at Abigail, her expression blank.

"What about this Emily person? Does she tell you things as well?"

"She throws up from the sea."

"Not that drivel," Abigail exclaimed.

"Yes, miss—ah, no, miss," Jacqueline stammered. "She tells me nothing."

"Well, mind that you tell her nothing further about me—or Miss Cunningham." Abigail stepped out of her frock. "If I hear any more gossip about me or my family from someone else, I shall be very angry."

Emily stood at the foot of their bunk with her back toward Jacqueline, trying to dry the tears streaming down her face with a handkerchief, to no avail. "By all that is holy, Miss Bordeaux," she said between sobs, "I told Mrs. Tibault nothing." Turning, she tried to look at Jacqueline directly, but was overwhelmed by her emotions. "I pray you, do not be angry with me," she cried. "I need you for my friend."

Arms folded across her chest, still furious, Jacqueline glared at her without speaking.

Emily's voice trembled as she continued, dabbing at her eyes. "How did you guess?"

Jacqueline hadn't the slightest notion what the girl was talking about. "Guess what?" she asked impatiently.

"Does it show already?"

"No more riddles, pray," Jacqueline exclaimed, her tone

an exact match for Abigail's when her patience had been exhausted.

Emily hung her head, and buried her face in her hands. "I am pregnant."

Amos Pettigrew loosened his tie and fumbled for the bottle of cognac he'd hidden under the mattress. Except for the midwatch, *The Seascape* was asleep, and it was time for some serious drinking. Alone. Rum before and wine at dinner had been absorbed by the meal, and a tot or two of brandy with a cigar was inadequate to produce the numbness he sought. Kicking off his boots to fall where they might, he flopped on his bed, pulled the cork, and, disdaining a glass, took a deep, satisfying pull.

Who would have thought that all of his midnights spent laboring over texts on anatomy would have come to this? Setting a seaman's broken finger. Smearing ointment on a stoker's scorched nose. Diagnosing a maid's pregnancy. Measuring out one-eighth gram of corrosive sublimate dissolved in fifteen drops of water with one-tenth gram of morphine acetate for ten consecutive days in a year so that he could inject it into the arm of the syphilitic vulgarian to whom he had sold his soul.

Worse than the boredom was the waiting. And watching. His silence bought and paid for. Knowing that the disease that had claimed Malcolm Tibault's first wife as surely doomed the second. Wondering if the poor young thing would be lucky enough to catch pneumonia.

▽

5

Aɴɢʀʏ, ᴛʜᴇ ᴍᴏᴜɴᴛᴀɪɴ god Pelee roared, spewing flames of sulfur skyward. Noxious fumes not dissipated by the wind drifted back down the sides of the volcano that had created the island of Martinique and fumigated the city of Saint-Pierre nestled at the edge of the wide bay on the northwest coast. But at the theater, a farce by Molière was in the offing that evening, and a real play performed by a professional troupe of actors was too tempting a diversion for the passengers of *The Seascape*, at anchor in the bay, to pass up on account of a mere smell.

Jacqueline was ecstatic. The handsome theater, with its dramatic facade of arches and delicately wrought-iron railings that decorated the twin curved stone stairways was reserved for the elite. But Abigail had flown in the face of protocol and insisted that her maid be allowed to attend, although she'd be confined to the third tier under the rafters. Gowned in neck-high somber colors, she could pass for a widow in her second year of mourning, which would account for her lack of jewels, yet permit her to venture out on an evening without censure. In deference to her hosts, Abigail conceded that it would be too awkward for Jacqueline to be ferried back and forth with her betters; therefore, her maid would travel in the cutter with the sailors and those other servants who had shore leave.

Jacqueline was so excited about an evening at the theater listening to her own language that she would have willingly swum the distance.

At first, only the Houdinis had openly approved Abigail's liberal stance. But when they tried to congratulate her, Abigail brushed their comments aside and confessed to having been entirely self-serving. Her French was even more sparse than Jacqueline's English, and Maude's nonexistent. While the actors would no doubt make themselves understood without language, she wanted an interpreter should she have any questions afterward.

Not to be outdone by a guest once he realized that Abigail was serious, Malcolm had volunteered Boris as an escort for Jacqueline, and it had been Abigail's turn to be discomfited. She resented his gesture, sensing that it smacked of paternalism. Further, she had no desire to place Jacqueline in the path of temptation. It would be unseemly to say the least if her maid were to become embroiled in a compromising situation with a valet from a household in which she was a guest. It would bespeak a woeful lack of control on her part. Better Jacqueline mate with Kinkade, if at all. Although it rankled, in the end she had to agree with Maude that sauce for the goose was sauce for the gander, and kept her objections to herself.

Except for the evening at the theater wherein all were to foregather in the high-vaulted gallery, for the week that the yacht was to be moored in the bay, her passengers were free to come and go as they pleased. Two coxswains and their cutters were on call at all times, and a third to accommodate the crew on a more regulated schedule.

With an entire day looming large to be filled, Abigail fairly itched to explore the island. Maude was not so enthusiastic, especially when she learned that as soon as the yacht had dropped anchor, two able-bodied seamen had lowered a large dinghy containing two diving dresses, and disappeared into the tangle of moored ships with Jeramy and Malcolm on board.

Preoccupied with duties that he might better have left with the sailing master to tend to had he not been so conscientious, Captain Thomas elected to stay on board. As did Mrs. Tibault, pleading a headache.

There was no question that Jacqueline had to remain on board to finish sewing her dress, but without her presence, there arose the delicate question of who would be chaperoning whom in the small party that was going ashore, because Mr. and Mrs. Houdini were not much for viewing churches and had expressed a desire to explore the island by themselves.

Amos Pettigrew was a most eligible bachelor, but his profession, and his very demeanor, somehow precluded his compromising any lady, including Abigail. Peter Tibault was an entirely different matter, and Abigail had to promise Maude that she'd take care not to find herself alone with him. Of course, no one would ever be so crude as to mention it, but Winifred Dupree was at least as old as Maude, and also a spinster. Therefore, it would be well within the bounds of propriety should she, or Maude for that matter, wander about the island with him.

Thus, after a stroll along the lovely tree-shaded street that led to the last church on their junket, when Peter decided to rest in the back pew, no one took exception when Winifred chose to remain with him while they examined the stained-glass windows.

Peter's expression was glum as he stood, hat in hand, waiting for Winifred to settle herself before sliding in beside her. Balancing his tall hat on his knee, he rested his hands upon the silver head of his walking stick and sighed heavily.

Winifred toyed with the ruffles on her folded parasol as she leaned close to whisper in his ear. "Mooning after your father's wife?" she asked in a tone filled with sarcasm.

"I rue the day you introduced me to her," he replied bitterly, staring at the retreating backs of Abigail, Maude, and Amos as they walked up the aisle toward the front of the church.

"You could not possibly regret it more than I, dear boy." Satisfied with the state of her parasol, she placed it across her lap. "Whatever possessed you to introduce her to your father?"

Peter ignored her question. "What do women see in him?" He shook his head in wonderment.

"You miss the point," she replied ruefully. "It is what he sees in women that attracts them."

"Humph!" Peter struck his cane on the floor. "All I see is a fickle beast of a girl that I could strangle with my bare hands."

"It is your father who needs strangling."

Placing his fingers to his lips, Peter warned her to keep her voice down. "Our luck has not changed, Miss Dupree." His tone was ironic as he nodded his head toward the front of the church where the doctor was pointing his walking stick at a stained-glass window while Abigail and Maude stood near hanging on his every word. "How can we plot murder with an avowed detective in our midst?"

"Piffle!" Winifred exclaimed contemptuously, unfurling her fan and placing it in front of her face to shield their conversation. "Miss Danforth's ambition is so much amusing dinner conversation. Whoever heard of such a thing as a detective, much less a girl being one?"

"Then you have not read much of Conan Doyle."

"I do not read at all," she replied, fanning herself in earnest. "Who has the time?"

Again, Peter sighed heavily. "Without her, I have nothing but time."

"Now, now, Mr. Tibault," Winifred said, not unkindly. "You will find another sweetheart by and by."

Peter twisted about to face her. "If it is so easy to replace the one you love, why have you not done so, pray?"

Her face crumpled. Had he slapped her, the effect could not have been more profound. Dropping her fan on top of the parasol in her lap, she opened the reticule that dangled from her wrist and pulled out a handkerchief.

Peter was immediately contrite. "I am so awfully sorry, Miss Dupree," he cried, patting his pockets in search of a handkerchief, which he failed to find before she retrieved hers. "I did not mean to upset you. Pray, forgive me."

"Oh, you are not to blame," she said, dabbing at her eyes. "It is that scoundrel father of yours."

"Perhaps you are right after all," Peter replied. As he looked toward the front of the church to see if anyone was paying attention to them, his gaze fell on Maude. "Perhaps my father does need killing before he harms anyone else," he continued, his voice a mere whisper so that he'd not be overheard.

But Maude was intent on Amos Pettigrew's lecture, as was Abigail, and all three were innocent of the commotion in the back of the church as they admired the leaded windows. As much as the craftsmanship and brilliant colors that the sun painted as it poured through the stained glass, they were spellbound by Amos's endless supply of stories that he swore were gospel regarding the violent history of skulduggery and piracy that had culminated in such beauty.

As for Amos, seldom did he have two such lovely ladies listening to his every word. He had certainly not expected Maude to be so attentive. The women to whom Malcolm was attracted were usually so smitten with him that they had no patience for anyone else even when he was not about, or they were so empty-headed that they had no patience for the appreciation of art or history. The Misses Danforth and Cunningham were of a different stripe, and they kept his toe to the mark with their questions that bespoke a genuine interest. So engrossed had he been that he'd quite lost track of the time, and as they turned away from the window to repair to the matching one on the other side of the church, he pulled his watch from its pocket. "Oh, my!" he exclaimed, snapping it shut and hastily replacing it. "I have quite forgot myself." Flustered by the lateness of the hour, he said, "I am afraid we must forgo the rest of the windows, ladies, and begin our journey back to the ship, lest you be late for curtain time." He gestured with his cane for Abigail and Maude to precede him up the aisle. "I apologize for being so long-winded."

"False modesty does not become you, sir," Abigail said as she consulted the watch pinned to the bodice of her linen suit. Also surprised by the time, she glanced at Maude, shrugged, and started toward the back of the church. "I have enjoyed your tales immensely, even though I confess I doubt the veracity of some," she said with a teasing smile.

"I agree with Miss Danforth on both counts, Dr. Pettigrew." As Maude fell into step beside Abigail, she turned slightly to speak to Amos as he brought up the rear. "Is there really more treasure on sunken ships surrounding the island than is to be found in all the churches?"

"Indubitably!" Amos exclaimed with a grin that deliberately left his voiced assurance in doubt.

"I must say I wish we did not have to hurry so," Abigail said plaintively.

"May I remind you that it is you who insisted upon having your maid attend the theater?" Maude asked with some asperity. "If she did not have to rush about helping Mrs. Tibault in the bargain, we might not have to rush so, either."

"Perhaps now that the ship is at anchor, Emily will be able to return to her duties tonight," Abigail said. "What is your opinion, Dr. Pettigrew?"

"I beg your pardon?" Amos blushed, the color spreading to his hairline.

"Did the wretched girl not consult you?" Abigail asked. Maude kept looking straight ahead, but Abigail glanced back at Amos when she addressed the question to him. She could not help but notice his disquiet, and it puzzled her.

"Ah . . . I really could not say," he stammered as he sought a reply that would not embarrass the ladies, or worse, betray a patient's confidence.

"I'll wager she confided his diagnosis in Jacqueline." Since Maude had not witnessed the doctor's discomfort, she spoke in an offhand manner.

"Perhaps she did at that." Relieved, hoping he was off the hook, Amos resisted the impulse to pull out his handkerchief and wipe his brow. Soon they'd be outside and he could restore his hat, and with luck the subject was done with.

It cost her dear, since she would have insisted that Jacqueline consult a physician immediately should she become incapacitated, but Abigail did not pursue the subject of Emily's health. She could tell that the good doctor did not wish to discuss his patient, and because he'd been so kind and entertaining, she had no desire to put him on the spot by prying. However, as they reached the back of the church, and Peter and Winifred stood to join them, she resolved to brace Jacqueline the moment she set foot on board the yacht.

Ariadne stood at the railing on the promenade deck of *The Seascape*. A wide-brimmed hat and parasol protected her face from the sun as she stared out to sea, deep in thought. Her disbelief at having caught the fancy of Peter's father had, in rapid succession, changed to surprise and then delight before shifting into a permanent, overweening pride of conquest. Her mother had often told her, and she believed implicitly, that she was not particularly pretty, that her best, most alluring features, were her doll-like quality and her eyes. And so it had come to pass that gentlemen had been drawn to her dainty helplessness by their own need to protect, and her eyes were such a deep blue that all who gazed into them were convinced that they could see something more in their depths than mere color.

To have snared a wealthy gentleman of the world the likes of Malcolm Tibault had been a coup. That he had a wife who lay dying even as he courted her bothered her not at all since he had made it clear that there had been little love lost between them—their marriage had been in name only for years, rendering him desperately lonely for companionship.

Where she had been content enough to have captured a wealthy man's son, she had soon begun to see Peter as his father saw him, a mere pup with little to teach her. When she also discovered that Peter would not inherit for another two years, and then only if he toed the mark, it had not taken her long to see where her best interests lay.

Malcolm had convinced her that, bereft of wifely companionship in his prime, it was only the sweet balm of her womanhood that could render him whole again. She could see that the competition for his favor was keen, including as it did her cousin Winifred, but knowing she'd lose him as well as her virginity if she succumbed to his importuning without benefit of matrimony, she had risked all and held out for a ceremony that would make their mating legal. Also knowing that if she'd not met him exactly when she had she'd not have had the opportunity to capture him at all, Ariadne had blessed all the stars in the firmament for placing her in the right place at the right time.

His courtship had been swift upon his wife's passing, but more swiftly still Ariadne had learned that being married to a rich man was a far cry from being courted by one, and it was an exceedingly uncomfortable bed that she found herself lying in. Literally. The sleepy-eyed manner in which Malcolm had gazed at her had turned her knees to jelly, and, far from dreading her wedding night, she had eagerly anticipated the pleasures he had promised with his eyes and veiled innuendos. Wine and his seductive glances at the small party after their wedding had sent her pulses racing, but once alone the entire event had been over in a trice, leaving her bewildered and disappointed. And sore. He, however, had been content afterward, or so she was left to assume since he had fallen asleep at once. She would never forget lying in the flickering candlelight that had seemed so romantic when he had entered the chamber to claim her, praying that drink had made him so impetuous and unheedful of her, and that their next mating would be less hurried.

But it was not to be. Fully clothed, and in public, or when there was no chance for consummation, Malcolm Tibault could make any woman believe he was the most skilled and ardent lover that it was her good fortune to meet. But once alone in the bedroom, he scarcely took time to bestow a kiss on the lips he had spent an entire evening gazing at hungrily, before he had completed his part of that most intimate of acts. Ariadne blamed herself for her lack of response.

As a single maiden, it had taken but a soulful glance and a mournful sigh to have new suitors vying for her attention.

Making a current lover jealous to bring him to heel had always been effective in the past. It never occurred to her that as Malcolm Tibault's wife the same ploy might not work. That she might be in over her head.

With but a skeleton crew on board, the stowaway stealthily ventured forth to stretch only to discover that the odor of sulfur that permeated the bay was not much of an improvement over the quality of air in the hold. He was not due to emerge until the morrow, and it would have been safer to wait until nightfall, but the soothing balm of sunlight beckoned irresistibly. Dressed as he was in a seaman's white garb, he was not likely to be noticed.

"No more churches, I pray you, Miss Cunningham," Abigail said as she shut the door to their stateroom and headed straight for the bell to summon Jacqueline.

"I thought you enjoyed Dr. Pettigrew's lecture, Miss Danforth," Maude replied with some surprise as she walked toward the birdcage. "At least you gave him every impression that you did," she added, poking a fingertip through the tiny bars to greet the singing bird. "Were you merely being polite?"

"Of course, I meant what I said." Abigail tugged at her gloves as she took the few steps to the dressing table. "Did you happen to notice how flustered he became when I mentioned Emily?"

Maude shrugged her denial. "Are you sure you are not imagining things?"

"Quite," Abigail replied firmly, dropping her gloves on the dressing table. "Why could he not just say she'd been seasick and was on the mend?"

Again, Maude shrugged. "Perhaps because she was not."

"But why the mystery?"

Maude turned her attention away from the canary to gaze at Abigail thoughtfully. When Jacqueline had first mentioned that Emily was throwing up, having had her own experience with morning sickness, it had crossed her mind that the poor girl just might be pregnant. But as intelligent as Abigail was, she was woefully ignorant in some matters. "You are the detective, can you not guess?" she asked, hoping that she'd not need to explain.

"You know I never guess," Abigail exclaimed, taking umbrage at the insult to her powers of deductive reasoning.

So engrossed were they that Jacqueline's soft knock escaped their notice, but when she let herself in, both turned to greet her.

"Then let Jacqueline tell us what is going on." Much relieved that she would not be the one to broach such an embarrassing subject, Maude swept her hand toward the tiny maid as if introducing a famous personage.

Jacqueline looked at her mistress expectantly.

"Is Emily on duty tonight?" Abigail asked.

"No, miss. I will tend Mrs. Tibault when I am excused from here."

"Then what is the matter with her?" she asked, not a little annoyed. "We are in port, the ship scarcely moves."

Jacqueline lowered her gaze, her face crimson.

Abigail turned to Maude, her expression a study in puzzlement.

"Since I do not mind admitting to the practice, might I hazard a guess?" Maude asked.

Abigail did not deign to answer but gestured with her hand as if granting permission.

Realizing the delicacy of situation she was embarking upon by prying, Maude's tone was gentle as she asked, "Might Emily be pregnant?"

"Miss Cunningham!" Abigail exclaimed, shocked.

Torn by conflicting loyalties, Jacqueline did not know what to say or do. But it soon occurred to her that as long as Maude knew the truth, she might as well admit it, and, after a swift glance at her mistress, she looked at Maude and gave an almost imperceptible nod.

Abigail gasped.

"And the father?" Maude asked. "Who is he?"

Jacqueline shrugged.

"She does not know who the father is?" Abigail asked, astonished. "How can that be?"

"If she bedded more than one man—" Maude began.

"Oh, no, Miss Cunningham," Jacqueline interrupted, shaking her head vehemently. "She knows. She does not tell me."

"Well, then, we have a little detective work ahead of us, do we not?" Abigail said, her expression grim.

"Miss Danforth," Maude exclaimed, shocked by Abigail's response. "You have no business whatever meddling in this affair."

Abigail said nothing, but set about untying the bow that anchored her hat. She was not about to defend herself in front of a servant, but neither was she going to allow a serving girl's life to be shattered if she could find the scoundrel who ruined her, and shame him into supporting her and his baby.

▽

6

THE EVENING AT the theater was less than successful. In Malcolm's case, perhaps the blame lay with his lack of success during the day. After the botheration of gearing up in the diving dress, his first dive had bored him and he'd been ready to return to *The Seascape* right then and there. Hoses attached to the helmet were supposed to pump in fresh air, but he'd no sooner found his feet upon the sea floor than the air had turned foul. The tiny windows had fogged over, severely limiting his vision, and even though the water was clear, what with the bubbles created by his spent breath and the churning sand stirred by his weighted boots, he could scarcely see the outlines of the sunken ship much less keep track of Jeramy, and watch his air hose as agreed.

Jeramy had been so intent on filling his sack with all manner of unidentifiable objects, he had been oblivious to any discomfort. Upon gaining the surface after their first descent, Jeramy's enthusiasm for the hunt was so great that Malcolm had allowed himself to be persuaded to stick it out. The avid treasure hunter had even offered to show him what to look for so that he could tell the difference between a worthless piece of barnacled timber and a heavily crusted object that, once cleaned, might prove to be a prize. No matter. He'd had no better luck in finding anything on subsequent dives.

Malcolm had to admit that the flurry of interest that his party had created upon entering the theater's high-vaulted gallery had pleased him. Aware of his own white-tie-and-tails splendor, he enjoyed the head-turning, admiring glances that his petite, gem-encrusted wife had attracted as she clung to his arm. Mounting the stairs, he had been surprised to see his friends, the LaSalles, in the milling crowd below, since he'd found his calling cards returned from them when he'd reached *The Seascape,* indicating that they were not receiving, and had assumed that they were away. He knew he had risked giving offense by marrying so swiftly after his wife's death, and as he turned to resume his progress up the stairs, he wondered if he might be the victim of a snub. The flurry of interest generated by their entrance soured and, ensconced in his box with the curtain going up, the unaccustomed activities of the day caught up with him. Not understanding one word of the dialogue, his heavy-lidded eyes grew heavier, and he seriously considered having Captain Thomas heave anchor at first light instead of staying the week.

This was Ariadne's first visit to Martinique. She had assumed that, except for the LaSalles, her husband had no friends in residence or he would have introduced her. Instead, he'd gone off on a mysterious errand with Jeramy Singleton after promising to show her where the Empress Josephine had been born on the morrow. She knew she looked exceptionally well. Jacqueline was far more talented with the curling iron than her own Emily, and she reveled in the impression she had created, both upon the crowd of strangers, and her husband, as she had entered the glittering gallery and swept up the stairs on his arm. She was mightily pleased with her exalted station in life, even though the diamonds sparkling at her throat scratched every time she moved her head.

Peter was by turns utterly bedazzled by Ariadne in the finery that his father had provided, and depressed anew by the knowledge that she was lost to him forever. He was careful to sit behind her and to the left so that her profile was in the path of his line of vision to the stage. There he could gaze at her to his heart's content with no one the wiser.

Like Maude, Winifred Dupree was not ordinarily privy to the services of a lady's maid. In honor of the evening at the theater, she had hoped to engage Emily to fix her hair in a fancier manner than she usually wore it, but when the girl had continued on the sick list, she had taken some extra time and managed an attractive, if plain, coiffure. But although she had made a most careful toilette and her gown was becoming, her modest necklace of topaz could not begin to compete with Ariadne Tibault's diamonds, which might have been hers. She felt like an old-maid frump, and ready to kill, only she could not decide if she'd rather see Ariadne, Peter, or his father dead. Even though Captain Perkins, resplendent in his uniform and medals, was serving as her escort, she was grateful for the shadows in the back of the box, which gave her some measure of privacy for her dark thoughts.

Although he tried to heed his wife's advice and enjoy an evening at the theater as part of the audience instead of being on stage, Houdini found it difficult to relax.

Having only recently forsworn widow's weeds, except for a brooch or two, Maude possessed no jewels worthy of an evening such as this and, at Abigail's insistence, had borrowed her garnets, even though the present company had seen the rightful owner wear them. It did not escape Maude's notice that while her escort for the evening might be rail thin, his shoulders were broad, which made his tails fit smashingly. However, Jeramy seemed subdued, and because she was a bit tired herself from all the touring and trips back and forth to the yacht, Maude was just as pleased that he did not seem to want to engage her in conversation.

Jeramy might have seemed subdued to Maude, but he was seething inside. He dared not allow his ill humor to show—the effort it took to conceal his turmoil also took its toll upon his usual easy charm—and he was grateful that Maude did not seem to require conversation. He had staked every penny he'd been able to scrape together to be on this cruise. He had left Panama without paying his bills and several tailors were the poorer for having outfitted him so grandly. But clothes made the man, and to keep up with the rich one had to wear the proper costumes. Yet, as the house lights dimmed, he was beginning to wonder if he'd made the right choice in gaining an uneasy berth on *The Seascape* instead of throwing in his lot with Philip and his battered schooner. Nor would he know until after this interminable evening was done. What to the rich man was a morning's diversion was Jeramy's only hope of garnering wealth. Even if he possessed a reliable map, it would take longer than one morning's worth of diving to harvest enough to set him up, unless he was extraordinarily lucky. So fascinated was he by the beauty under water and its promise of untold treasure, it had never occurred to him that Peter's father would not be as enthralled. But after a single dive, they would have returned to the yacht had he not insisted that they stay. Tomorrow he would take Peter with him, or go alone, and be damned if his host did not approve.

Amos Pettigrew was pressed into service as Abigail's escort, a chore he performed reluctantly, although he concealed his trepidation with flawless manners. He knew that Emily confined herself to her bed, and, given Abigail's overweening curiosity, he was not sure how he would handle it were she to press him for a diagnosis. But even as the lights dimmed, she still had not made an inquiry, and he began to hope that she had forgotten all about the maid, at least for the nonce. As the curtain rose, it suddenly occurred to him that Abigail might be aware of the untenable spot she would put him in by prying, and therefore had curbed her curiosity. Such self-control was not common even among well-bred gentlemen when they had a bit in their teeth, and a new respect for the young girl who was lovely in blue, took root.

Sapphires, encircled by tiny, faceted diamonds graced the décolletage created by Abigail's gown of matching blue taffeta. She did not care overmuch for bedecking herself with jewels, but, having inherited some fine pieces from her mother, did so when the occasion warranted. Yet even as she conformed to society's demands, she had shuddered inwardly while observing the effect of the Tibaults' entrance, with Ariadne decorated like a Christmas tree clinging to her husband's arm. She proclaimed his wealth with her lavish gown and as many costly baubles as could be displayed on her tiny person and still remain within the bounds of fashion. Ariadne was living the very lifestyle Abigail disdained, yet she admired the young wife for the stoic manner in which she bore her trials. It was not often that her feelings were thus inconsistent, and she found it unsettling.

Even as the curtain went up and the play began, her troubled thoughts continued to stray. Travel was supposed to be broadening, yet it would seem that the more she saw of the world, the less she understood, which was in itself another paradox. Emily's predicament was a real puzzlement. While Abigail might be innocent of the details, she was full aware that babies resulted from lewd behavior between the sexes. And it was common knowledge that many a dollymop entered service in a great house for the express purpose of luring the young master into an indiscretion, thereby trapping him into matrimony. Abigail had always wondered why any girl with a drop of sense would try such a ploy. The consequences were much more likely to be disastrous, since any servant girl discovered to be with child was invariably dismissed out of hand, without references, making it impossible for her to gain another position. What else could follow but destitution? Never before had she questioned that such a temptress deserved to be punished, if not for the deed, then for her stupidity.

But now that she was faced with an actual situation instead of theory, Abigail was struck by the question of what would happen to the baby. Was it to be punished also? Yet, except for being born, it was innocent of any wrongdoing, and it occurred to her that a punishment that had seemed to fit the crime was too harsh when it splashed over onto the innocent. Nor did it seem altogether fair since it clearly took two people to cooperate in some fashion to produce a baby. Since the very foundation of society rested on the fact that only the man was allowed to be the breadwinner and responsible for supporting his children, how could he be so careless about begetting them? Also, it would seem that any gentleman worthy of the name should be able to resist temptation, or at the very least having succumbed, take some responsibility for his weakness should it produce one of his progeny. Furthermore, and most curious of all, he was more likely to make his conquest an honest woman if she were someone of his own class. But if it were a matter of class difference, why would any gentleman risk starting an heir with an improper mother? Or could it be that because she was daring to support herself, however meagerly, that a servant was exempt from his gallantry?

It was all too much. Solving a murder was not nearly so slippery a task as trying to make sense out of society's thicket of unwritten rules, and she could almost wish she had a real crime to occupy her thoughts instead. Swiftly chastising herself for wishing anyone killed, however fleetingly, merely to distract her from some difficult thinking, she turned her attention to the play. But not until she had resolved to escape those who would chaperon her at intermission, and have a word with Peter. Perhaps if she were clever enough to catch him off-guard and watch his reactions closely, she could detect if he were indeed the father.

In all the years the Tibaults had been coming to Martinique, Boris had never been in this theater. True, he was not understanding one word of the play, but the acting was so broad, and with Jacqueline's help with a word or two, he was understanding the action perfectly, and by the time intermission arrived he was enjoying himself hugely. It was with a good deal of gratitude toward her mistress that he escorted Jacqueline to the railing for a better view of the people below.

Jacqueline could scarcely catch her breath from excitement. The theater. The play. Her escort. The clothes. She devoted her life to fashion, yet as she looked down from the third-tier balcony she realized that this was the first time she had seen so much finery in one place. As the women milled about, their jewels, set alight by the chandeliers, twinkled like stars. Their gentlemen escorts were all black and white perfection, and she might have been in Paris for all the small talk she overheard around her. Yet, until now, she'd not had the opportunity to speak to Boris alone, and she could not waste the chance on mere chatter about fripperies. "I pray you, *monsieur*." Rather than look him in the eye, she kept her gaze upon the passing parade below. "Might I ask your advice on a matter most urgent to me?"

"It would do me great honor to be of service to you, Miss Bordeaux," Boris said, feeling expansive.

"Can you keep the secret?" she asked with a quick glance to note his response.

He shrugged. "As well as most."

It was not as good as a sincere crossing of the heart, but Jacqueline was so in need of counsel she decided that it would do. "Mrs. Tibault asks me to take Emily's place," she whispered. "I want to know does she do this before?"

"Hmmmm." Boris also watched the crowd below. He was silent so long, Jacqueline began to wonder if he'd heard her. "To answer your question, Miss Bordeaux," he said, just as she opened her mouth to speak again, "I am not surprised."

"Oh?" Eager to match his casualness, Jacqueline refrained from saying anything further.

"Emily belonged to the first Mrs. Tibault . . . and besides you are French."

"The second Mrs. Tibault could have her choice of any girl on this island, or any other island." Jacqueline waved her hand to indicate the outside world. "Why me?"

"Ah, but you are the genuine article from Paris. Miss Danforth is exceptionally well traveled, and is always turned out perfectly due to your talents. Luring you away would be a coup." He paused before adding, "She is sure to be up and around soon, is she not?"

Even though she was certain that no one they knew was

nearby, Jacqueline glanced around before asking, "Can you keep another secret?"

Again, he merely shrugged.

Jacqueline would have preferred something more firm by way of a promise since the secret was someone else's, but she was pressed. "Emily is with child," she said, her voice grave.

"Is that so?" His tone was noncommittal.

"I worry because she threatens suicide." She shot a swift, sideways glance at him. "She will not say who is the father."

"Do not look at me!" His laugh was harsh. "She would not come near the likes of me." But it was not because he had not tried, and he was delighted to hear that miss prim-and-proper had gotten her comeuppance. As the gong signaled the end of intermission, it was with some glee at the news that he took Jacqueline by the elbow to escort her back to their seats.

For insular communities such as Martinique, intermissions at the theater were as much a part of the performance as the play and occasionally provided more drama as when the LaSalles looked straight at, and then through, the Tibaults as the couples passed one another on the first-tier promenade. Ariadne was oblivious to the snub but it set Malcolm to seething, and he promptly resolved to pull anchor at first light. It did nothing to sweeten his humor when, just as the first gong sounded signaling the end of intermission, Amos slipped him a note requesting an interview when they returned to the yacht.

Amos took his role as Abigail's escort seriously, and it was only when he excused himself to speak briefly to Malcolm that Abigail was free to turn to Peter, who was standing directly behind her, and say, "I wonder if I might ask you a question, Mr. Tibault."

"Ask anything you like, Miss Danforth," he replied graciously. Curious, he drew closer, the better to hear her over the din of the crowd milling about.

Abigail unfurled her fan to create a pocket of privacy

between them before continuing. "Would you mind telling me how long Emily has been in your stepmother's employ?" Taking advantage of the necessity of staying close to hear his response, she watched his face carefully.

"I really could not say, Miss Danforth." He shrugged nonchalantly. "My mother hired her when I was away." He paused only briefly before adding, "Might I now play turn-about and ask why you wish to know?"

To mask the ulterior purpose, Abigail was careful to speak with more annoyance in her tone than she actually felt. "It struck me as odd why she would be employed on a cruise if it were known that she was prone to seasickness."

A sensitive young man, Peter picked up the anger in her voice and responded to what he perceived to be the cause of the emotion. "Oh, I say," he said sincerely. "You must have been dreadfully inconvenienced, Miss Danforth, deprived of your maid's full attention and all." He sighed, and shrugged again. "Alas, but again I cannot help you, I am sorry to say." His eyes grew sad, and he suddenly looked away. "I seldom traveled with my parents."

Abigail had no chance to further the conversation because Amos had returned to her side to escort her to her seat, but she had heard enough to convince her that Peter was innocent. And then her heart sank to her boots as the next logical culprit occurred to her. Malcolm. But if that be the case, wherefore Maude's infatuation? Worse still, she could feel her resolve to brace the cad weaken. Perhaps it would be best to simply feign an illness in Havana and quit the cruise.

"This had better be good, Pettigrew." Much like a caged animal, still dressed in his evening clothes, Malcolm Tibault paced back and forth in the doctor's small stateroom, annoyed at being summoned like a schoolboy to the principal's office. "Why the urgency?" he asked impatiently.

Amos sat in the chair to allow Malcolm more room to pace. "Mrs. Tibault's maid is pregnant," he said, his voice flat.

Malcolm stopped in his tracks. His eyes were mere slits as he looked down at Amos. "Why are you telling me this?"

Amos stared up at him. "Would you prefer that I tell Mrs. Tibault?" he asked, careful to keep the sarcasm from his tone.

"Damn!" Malcolm whirled away to resume his pacing. "Well, of course, the girl must be let go."

Amos waited until Malcolm was on the return trip before asking, "Is it yours?"

Malcolm stopped to look directly at him, again his gaze piercing. "Did she tell you it was?"

"Did you bed her?"

Malcolm flung his arms wide. "So did half the ship's complement for all I know." Turning, he resumed his pacing.

"Damn it, man," Amos exclaimed. "There is more at stake here than a girl's reputation. If it is your baby, it could be born blind, or witless, or hideously deformed."

"Perhaps it is not mine."

"Perhaps it is."

"Did she tell you that?"

Amos fell silent.

Malcolm stood over him. "Did she?" he insisted.

Amos shrugged. "She refused to tell me anything."

"Aha!" Malcolm exclaimed triumphantly. "Then you do not know with any certainty, do you?"

"Damn it, Tibault!" Amos said, near the end of his patience. "Did you have carnal relations with her, or not?"

"What does it matter what I say if the slut will not tell you who the father is? More than likely she does not know!"

"It matters if you are spreading the disease!"

"I do not have to answer to you or anyone else!" Malcolm exclaimed, drawing himself up to his full height.

"If you would only wear a condom, none of this would happen."

"Come on, Amos, you know perfectly well you cannot feel a damned thing through all that rubber." Malcolm took the few steps necessary to reach the door before turning to face the doctor. "I would just as soon have a bowel movement for all the sensation you get wearing one of those."

"Are you saying that you do not protect your own wife?" Amos could not conceal his horror.

"You had better not be trying to tell me how to run my life," Malcolm said ominously, his hand on the doorknob. "I pay you handsomely to forget what you know." Opening the door, he stalked out.

"You bastard!" Amos shouted—after the door was safely shut.

$\triangledown$

7

INTENT ON THE delicate task of chipping away the crust
and grime of ages from the objects that Jeramy had rescued
from the deep, both he and Peter were oblivious to the
natural creaks and moans of the ship as she lay calm in the
harbor. Nor did they notice the wildly gyrating shadows on
the walls and ceiling of Jeramy's cabin, cast by the flickering
light from the kerosene lamp that lit their efforts.

Neither man had slept a wink, and Peter was strung tight
with suspense. Both had worked through the predawn hours
after their evening at the theater, to no avail. They had taken
care to treat each piece drawn from the sack with great
tenderness in case it turned out to be a relic of value. Except
for three silver coins worth less than a sailor's monthly
money, all had either shattered into pebbles or revealed a
core of impenetrable rock.

Peter watched Jeramy's every move as the treasure hunter
tenderly picked the last bit of debris from the last piece,
which was the right size to be a snuff box. But most
important, the promising square chunk had not only re-
tained its shape, it had not shattered. Jeramy's hopes had
been dashed too many times, and he had refused to comment on this piece until it was clean enough to see what it
was.

Even though he could sense Jeramy's mounting excitement, Peter scarcely dared hope that his verdict would
be positive, but after a final, gentle brushing, Jeramy
held an oblong object, the top of which was covered with

rounded gems cut smooth, en cabochon, up to the light.

"Oh, my God and little green tadpoles," Jeramy whispered reverently. Eyes gleaming with triumph, he turned to Peter with a smile big enough to split his face in two.

"What is it?" Peter held his breath.

"It is one of Empress Josephine's snuff boxes."

"A snuff box?" Peter asked, unable to hide his disappointment.

"I would stake my life on it," Jeramy replied, crossing himself.

"What is so wonderful about a stupid snuff box, pray tell?"

"If it is part of the Empress Josephine's collection, which was lost when the frigate carrying it went down on the very spot where I was diving this morning, it is worth a great deal."

"We are rich!" Peter sprang from his chair and began cavorting about the tiny cabin. "We are rich!" Stopping to bend over Jeramy, who had remained seated, staring at the small box in his palm, Peter pounded on the treasure hunter's shoulders. "Did I not tell you to throw in your lot with me?" he exulted.

"And there is more where this came from," Jeramy said, his eyes aglow from the lamp, and his dreams. "Much, much more."

"Do you realize what this means?" Peter did not wait for an answer before darting away. "Father can go to hell," he exclaimed, jumping up and down. "I am rich!"

"Whoa! Peter, not so fast." Jeramy held out a restraining hand. "This is a minor box only—"

"What do you mean, minor box?" Peter stopped his jumping about to glare angrily at Jeramy. "Did you not just say the snuff boxes were worth a great deal?"

"Oh, this one is worth plenty, I assure you," Jeramy said. "After all, it belonged to the empress." Careful to keep his contempt for Peter's naivete from his voice, he added, "But more than that, it confirms that her lost collection must be nearby." As he pulled a handkerchief from the pocket of his trousers, he cast a shrewd glance at the young man standing in the shadows. Considering his options carefully, as he wrapped the box in the clean white square of cotton, he concluded that Peter's support would still be useful, and that it might be wise to hedge a bit. "Actually, it is not altogether a good sign that I found only one box, since the collection is supposed to be all together in a special chest."

His hopes fading fast, Peter immediately assumed the worst. "Do you think that somebody has already found the chest?" he asked anxiously.

"I would prefer to believe that it was somehow broken or rotted or nonexistent." Peter shrugged. "All I know for certain is that I need to make more dives if I am to recover anything at all."

"Will six days be enough time?" Peter asked, drawing close to the table again. "Once Father has set a schedule, he is not likely to change it, and he has promised to have the Houdinis in Havana by Christmas Eve."

"If I have not found them in six days, we will jump ship, old pal," Jeramy said expansively. "There were dozens in her collection. It is said that one box is completely covered in diamonds, and another carved from one huge emerald."

The anchor that held *The Seascape* snug in the harbor was abaft the beam, and since Jeramy's quarters were well forward, neither man had heard any of the attendant noise when it was hauled in. But when the engine coughed and rattled into life, setting the entire ship aquiver with its power, it awakened even the deepest sleeper aboard. Stunned, knowing instantly what had befallen them, Jeramy and Peter froze, staring at each other.

Peter was the first to break their shocked tableau. "Oh, my God, no!" he cried.

"We are under way!" Jeramy exclaimed incredulously. "Why are we moving?"

"Father!" Turning on his heel, Peter threw open the door and dashed for the companionway.

Jamming the snuff box into his trousers pocket, Jeramy followed close behind.

Neither man paid the slightest attention to the pink and orange sunrise when they gained topside. They dashed straight for the wheelhouse where, wild-eyed and unshaven, white ties discarded, shirts indecently unbuttoned, elegant tails woefully out of place in the dawning light, they found themselves most unwelcome.

The normally courteous Captain Perkins made short shrift of their entreaties, and threatened to have them escorted from the bridge forthwith by two large officers who stood ready nearby, if they did not quit it in peace at once. He was shipping out under orders, and if Peter knew what was good for him, he would not question his father's decision.

Realizing that Captain Perkins would be powerless to do anything but obey his father, Peter grabbed Jeramy by the arm, and the two sped from the wheelhouse as rapidly as they had gained it. However, he was entirely too wrought up to heed the captain's counsel not to disturb his father, and made straightaway for his luxurious quarters with Jeramy trailing behind. So upset was he that he cared not at all who he awakened as he pounded on the door.

Even though he knew his father's sitting room was heavily carpeted, he could not resist putting his ear to the door to try and hear if someone was approaching. Nothing. Doubling both hands into fists, he beat on the door harder. He stopped, and was about to put his ear to the door again when it opened a crack and his father peeked out.

"Oh, it is you," Malcolm said in disgust. Before he could close the door, Peter shoved against it hard enough to gain entrance.

"How dare you!" Malcolm said, backing away, too surprised by his son's sudden show of force to retaliate.

Peter drew the door closed behind himself, leaving Jeramy no choice but to remain in the corridor. "Why are we leaving Martinique?"

"None of your damn business." With the utmost insouciance, Malcolm tied the sash to his satin dressing gown as he casually strolled to stand in the middle of the large sitting room—as if his son came bursting in looking like he'd escaped from a barroom brawl, at dawn every morning.

"You said we would stay for a week!"

"I changed my mind," Malcolm replied coolly. "Must I keep reminding you that I pay the bills here? I run things my way."

Peter wilted. A familiar feeling of helplessness crept over him, and he wished he were anywhere else on earth except standing before his father, begging for the impossible again.

"You might as well sit down as long as you are here," Malcolm said, gesturing toward the tufted settee. Moving to the bellpull, he asked, "Shall I ring for coffee? You look like you could use some."

Relieved that his father did not seem angry, and completely disarmed by his rare display of kindness, Peter refused the offer of coffee with a shake of his head, but gratefully sank down on the settee.

Malcolm remained standing. "Actually I am glad you . . . ah . . . dropped in. There is something I need to speak with you about."

Not knowing what to say, Peter shrugged, waiting with absolute certainty that his father would continue.

"I will get straight to the point," Malcolm said. "Have you bedded my wife's maid?" he asked with a knowing smile.

Peter was flabbergasted. Not once in his entire life had his father so much as broached the subject of sex. "I beg your pardon, sir?" he managed to stammer.

With the smirk still in place, Malcolm spoke in a conspiratorial manner, one man to another. "It seems that Emily is with child and will not reveal who the father is." He shrugged in a knowing manner. "I was curious to know if you have been sleeping with her."

Peter was on his feet in a trice. "I do not sleep with servant girls, sir," he cried, shaking an angry fist at his father. "I promised my mother I would not pick up that despicable habit from you."

"Little bastard," Malcolm exclaimed, casting a glance about the room for something to strike Peter with. "How dare you talk to me like that!"

The glance was not lost on Peter, and he edged his way toward the door, but the sting from the insult to his character gave him the nerve to say, "How dare you leave Martinique with no warning."

"If you want to stay so badly, jump overboard and swim."

Peter had his hand on the door handle when he had an impulse to try a tack that sometimes worked when he wished to get something from his father that he was unwilling to bestow. "Oh I pray you, Father," he said, turning to face Malcolm. "Order Captain Perkins to turn about."

"Why?" Suddenly curious, Malcolm looked at his son quizzically. "Why should I turn back because of you?"

Completely unprepared for the question, Peter suddenly realized that he would have to confess his part in the matter of bringing a treasure hunter along on this cruise in the first place. Deciding that he'd best leave quickly, he grabbed the door handle again.

"Oh no you don't." Malcolm put his back to the door, blocking Peter's exit. "I insist." Reaching for one of his walking sticks in a ceramic jar by the door, he pulled it free. "Tell me why you broke in here, or I shall thrash you within an inch of your life."

Wide-eyed with a fear that rendered him speechless, Peter backed away from the door and the familiar menace of the upheld cane.

Enraged by his son's refusal to answer him, Malcolm raised the stick high and brought it down with all his might on Peter's shoulder. "How dare you." Malcolm grunted with the impact of the cane as it struck. Raising it again to strike Peter's other shoulder, he cried, "I will teach you to keep secrets from me!"

Peter flung his arms up to shield his head as best he could.

"Oh, I pray you, no more!" he cried. Younger and stronger than his father, he might have wrenched the weapon from Malcolm's hands, and turned the tables, but too many childhood beatings had robbed him of the will to strike back. Covering his head with his hands, he fell to his knees and cowered on the floor.

Malcolm stood above him, cane held high as if to deliver yet another blow. "Speak, you . . . you . . . coward!" And truth be told he heartily wished his son would speak, since he was exhausted from the unaccustomed exertion.

"Mr. Singleton found one of Empress Josephine's snuff boxes," Peter replied swiftly, hoping to stop the beating. "He is certain that the rest of the collection is buried nearby. He needs to dive again to find out."

Malcolm lowered the cane and poked Peter in his side with the tip, urging him to lower his hands from his head. "And how do you happen to be privy to this when it was I he took diving with him?"

Again, terror rendered Peter speechless. He knew if he could just pretend he was unafraid and in no pain from the beating, his father would relent, but he could only lie upon the carpet, bruises from the blows throbbing.

Malcolm poked him in the ribs again, not so gently. "Well?" he insisted.

Peter moaned. Breathing deep, he regained enough composure to continue calmly. "It is I who arranged for Mr. Singleton to meet you," he said, covering his head again in anticipation of more blows.

"What is that you say?" Malcolm had heard Peter perfectly well, he just could not believe that his son had the wherewithal to deceive him.

"It was no fortuitous accident that you met Mr. Singleton," Peter said, his voice quivering. "I arranged it."

"So having a treasure hunter aboard was your idea?" Malcolm was astonished, and almost pleased that his son had shown some gumption at last, even if it was at his expense.

Realizing that no further blows were coming, Peter slowly lowered his hands and, glancing up at his father, nodded without speaking.

"Hah!" Malcolm held the cane high, but instead of striking his son, he turned and thrust it into the jar with the others. "I would that you would admit that introducing your fiancée to me had been a setup."

Horrified, Peter uncoiled from his fetal position and looked up at his father. Had the beating continued he could not have been more appalled.

"Alas, I rue the day that I met her," Malcolm said as he crossed the room and slumped into the overstuffed chair by the settee. "Never mind that I married her."

"You cannot mean that, sir." Peter sat up as he spoke. "She is the dearest girl in all the world."

"And a crashing bore in bed. Just like all the rest. Soon as we reach Louisiana, I intend to divorce her. The Napoleonic Code is in force there. She'll not get a dime."

Peter was so horrified by his father's words, and the determination with which he spoke, that he quite forgot the beating he had just earned by contradicting him. "You cannot do that, sir," he said, gaining his feet. "She would be ruined!"

"Careful, boy," Malcolm said ominously, glaring up at his son.

Grateful that the caning had ended as swiftly as it had with no bruises that would show, Peter kept his peace.

"And where is this erstwhile treasure hunter now?" Malcolm asked.

Peter gestured toward the corridor.

"Well fetch him." Malcolm waved an impatient hand at the door. "I would have a word with him."

Brushing himself off as he moved to the door, Peter opened it to peer into the corridor.

With his ear to the door, Jeramy had heard the commotion inside, and knowing that Peter was coming to fetch him, stood square in the doorway. He might be slender, but confident of his strength he was determined to strike back should Malcolm attack him.

He no sooner entered the room than Malcolm spoke. "My son tells me you found the Empress Josephine's snuff box," he said, delivering an unspoken insult by remaining seated rather than standing to greet a guest to his suite.

Jeramy glanced at Peter. "Why are we leaving Martinique?"

"Our departure is none of your affair."

"But there is much treasure to be found."

"You told me nothing of the possibility of finding such a treasure." Malcolm looked from one man to the other with an exaggerated expression of innocence.

"I did not wish to get your hopes up, sir."

"My hopes?" Malcolm raked Jeramy with a scornful glance. "I had no hopes of finding anything. I thought diving might provide a morning's diversion." He shuddered. "I discovered that I despise it."

"I will do all the diving, sir," Jeramy said eagerly. "You need not descend again."

"If you want to stay so badly, I should have you thrown overboard!"

"No, Father!" Peter cried, knowing Malcolm to be quite capable of the deed.

"Oh, shut up, boy," Malcolm said contemptuously. "One more word from you and I shall have you tossed over the stern with the garbage."

"But if we stayed I could make you enormously rich," Jeramy exclaimed.

"I am already enormously rich."

"But—"

"Do not continue to insult me, Mr. Singleton." Malcolm lost patience. "It is not my wealth you wish to increase, but your own."

"But only by a small portion compared to yours."

"Oh, I pray you, Father, please turn about."

"Enough!" Malcolm shouted. "After you duped me you

expect me to grant you a wish?" He held his hand out. "I would like to see this snuff box."

"I do not have it with me," Jeramy lied.

"Then go and fetch it at once."

"I should say not." Jeramy backed away a step.

"The box is mine," Malcolm said. "I paid for it—and dearly, too."

"But I found it—" Jeramy began.

"Let me be clear," Malcolm said, looking Jeramy straight in the eye. "Either you fetch that snuff box and bring it to me at once, or I shall have six able-bodied seamen escort you to your cabin, and search it—and you. I assure you the experience will be most unpleasant."

Chin high, Jeramy glanced at Peter.

"I warn you," Malcolm continued. "Defy me and you will find yourself searching for treasure without a diving dress. I assure you, you would not be missed, nor would the authorities question your disappearance."

"You had better do as he says, Mr. Singleton," Peter said, his voice faint.

Duly impressed that Malcolm would make such threat in front of a witness, Jeramy reluctantly dug into the pocket of his trousers and handed over the handkerchief-wrapped box.

As Jeramy and Peter looked on hungrily, Malcolm unwrapped the box. After a cursory glance, unimpressed, he wadded it back up in the handkerchief and tucked it into the pocket of his dressing gown.

"Oh, sir, there is so much more where that came from," Jeramy cried, his hands spread in supplication.

"My orders are to head straightaway for Cuba. Had I not given my word to drop the Houdinis off there, we would be upon a steady course for the Gulf Coast."

"But, Father—what of San Juan or Kingston?"

"I have had enough of these filthy islands." Malcolm stood, and with a wave of his hand indicated that their interview was at an end.

"At least let me have a rowboat, and my gear," Jeramy said, as Peter reached for the door. "I will row back!"

Malcolm looked at both men scornfully. "If you wish to stay in Martinique that badly, you have my permission to jump."

Ariadne was chilled to the bone. She'd had no time to don a dressing gown over her nightdress when her husband had left their bed to respond to the thumping on the door, nor had she been willing to leave her position at the door to the sitting room to fetch one. Dashing across the bedchamber, she slipped into bed, drew the covers high, and feigned sleep.

Well fed for once and pleasantly weary from his day topside, the stowaway was enjoying the soundest sleep he'd had since the voyage began, until the engine kicked in. Waking with a start, he thought he might be dreaming. He could see nothing in the pitch black, but there was no mistaking the motion of the ship as she made way.

And then he knew he must be having a nightmare. They were leaving Martinique. But the whole point of his being on board was for the diving in the bay. Frantic, he could not even pace about in his agitation. Trapped like an animal, he could but stare into the darkness. And wait.

$\triangledown$

8

AWAKENED BY THE racket as the engine surged into power, Abigail raised herself up on one elbow. The stateroom was pitch black with curtains blocking the portholes. Nonetheless she peered into the darkness to try and see if Maude had been awakened also. Her sight no use, she listened intently but could not hear Maude's breathing over the hum and vibration of the engine, and assumed that the laudanum Maude was fond of taking at bedtime to ensure a sound sleep was having its effect. She knew immediately that they were under way—there was no mistaking that throb and rumble, and, of course, the motion of the ship itself.

Curious, she threw back the covers and, disregarding slippers and dressing gown, hands outstretched against bumping into the chair, groped her way to the portholes. She reached them with only a minor misstep into the birdcage, which elicited a sleepy chirp from the canary. Drawing back the curtains, she blinked at the pink and orange sky. And wondered why they were leaving Martinique so precipitously.

Carlotta did not know the why of it either when she brought their morning tea, only that *Señor* Tibault had given orders that they depart for Havana at first light. There would be no ports of call in between.

Nor had Jacqueline heard anything. She had readied Mrs. Tibault for sleep, to be true, but nary a word had been said about departing Martinique so soon. Her only news was that Emily would be resuming her duties today. Having readied her mistress for the morning, Jacqueline was about to take her leave when Maude, impatient with Abigail for not having done so during her toilette, baldly asked the tiny maid if Boris were the father.

"Miss Cunningham!" Abigail exclaimed reprovingly. Although she had her own theory, she hoped that Jacqueline might have gleaned something different from Boris, if she would tell. But she recognized the grim line that Jacqueline's mouth formed, and sought to circumvent a flat denial. "Jacqueline is not the detective. I am!"

Immediately aware of Abigail's ploy to get Jacqueline to talk, Maude shrugged, and sighed as if Abigail had spoken an unfortunate truth, and cast a sly glance at Jacqueline.

Fearing she'd be branded a Paul Pry, Jacqueline was about to deny having spoken to Boris about such a delicate matter, but could not resist Abigail's challenge. "He says not, Miss Danforth," she replied. The faintest hint of pride crept into her voice as she added, "He says she prefers her betters, and would have nothing to do with the likes of him." Since both Abigail and Maude were suddenly paying such strict attention to her words, she dared to add, "If you were to ask me, I think he is happy it happens to her." And with that, she curtsied and left.

Maude waited until the door was safely shut behind her before speaking. "Then it must be Peter," she said, drawing on her gloves.

"I think not," Abigail responded. "I had occasion to test the waters as it were, at intermission."

"Who then?"

"Oh, Miss Cunningham," Abigail said, with a reproving shake of her head. "How is it that you can be so blind?"

Maude drew herself tall. "What are you trying to say?"

"Malcolm Tibault must be the father."

Maude was outraged. "How dare you accuse him," she cried, an angry frown creasing her brow.

Abigail shook her head in wonderment. If ever she needed a reason not to allow emotion to interfere with her judgment, there it stood before her. Maude seemed utterly blind to the perfidy of their host. Or was she deliberately refusing to see? "He is the logical choice," she replied firmly.

"It could be anyone." Maude waved her hand about, indicating the rest of the ship. "There are dozens of sailors!" she cried. "Lovers on shore. How can you be so certain it was Mr. Tibault?"

"You heard Jacqueline as well as I," Abigail persisted. "Emily prefers her betters."

"You would value the word of servants over mine?" Maude glared at Abigail, insulted to the quick. "You know nothing of such matters," she said scornfully.

"I know all I need to know."

"You know nothing of matters of the heart."

"Ah, but I know a good deal about character, Miss Cunningham," Abigail replied. "Having married a girl half his age when his wife's body was not cold in its grave, it is clear that our host has none."

"You are quite impossible, Miss Danforth," Maude said, gathering her fan and reticule. As intelligent as Abigail was, there were times when her youth and emotional naivete were difficult to bear, and to be criticized by someone who knew nothing of which she spoke was intolerable. "If you will forgive me, I do believe I shall forgo our promenade this morning." Maude placed her hand on the doorknob, ready to exit. "I think it wise I take my constitutional alone lest I say something I shall regret." Not waiting to give Abigail a chance to respond, she opened the door and was gone.

Paneled in precious woods burnished to a high luster, Malcolm Tibault's study was an elegant room with bookcases lining one wall. He seldom read, but he knew their very presence convinced others that he did, and he inhabited the room much like he wore his clothes, using its magnificence to impress, intimidate, or seduce as the case may be. At the moment, as Emily sat on the edge of the chair across from his desk, he was attempting to do a bit of all three.

"Oh, but sir," she cried, wringing her hands, "you cannot mean to abandon me."

"How do I know you are telling the truth?" He shrugged nonchalantly.

"You know I was untouched until you had your way with me." Emily gestured toward the settee. "On that very sofa."

"I know no such thing." Slowly, Malcolm rose from the chair behind his desk. "You had the opportunity to sleep with anyone," he said, sauntering around it to stand over her.

She dared not gaze up at him. "You said it would be my job if I did not." Her voice trembled with fear.

"I think I have every right to assume that if you lay with me, you would lie with anyone," he said, toying with the lace on her cap. His heavy-lidded eyes raked her with a speculative glance.

Emily pulled away from his touch. "And what about you, Mr. Tibault?" She rose from the chair and moved so that it was between them. "I see how you look at that Miss Cunningham."

"She is a real lady," he said, strolling back to stand behind his desk. "You are little better than a harlot."

"You cad," she exclaimed, shaking her fist at him. "You know that is not true." Even as she protested, she realized there was a grain of truth in his words. Were she truly pure in heart, she would not have succumbed to his blandishments. She sank to the edge of the chair once again. "Oh, what am I to do?" She began to cry, burying her face in her hands.

Waiting a moment until her sobs had quieted somewhat, Malcolm spoke. "Why do you not have Pettigrew take care of it?"

She lifted her face out of her hands to glance at him. "What do you mean?"

"You know." He shrugged. "Get rid of it."

"Kill my baby?" She could scarcely say the words.

"Very well, then. If you insist." He sat down heavily. "I shall put you off the ship in Havana with the Houdinis.

Because of your long service with the first Mrs. Tibault, I will give you a little money, but you must promise never to come around asking for more."

"But I know no one in Cuba," she cried. "I speak no Spanish." Standing, she leaned across the desk. Hands clasped together, she pleaded with him. "Oh, I pray you, Mr. Tibault, at least take me to the mainland."

He shrugged. "Only if you swear you will stop accusing me of being the father of your bastard."

With little choice but to swallow her despair, Emily nodded.

Her relationship with Maude in disarray, Abigail had been delighted that the cruise was being cut short. But as the day progressed, it became clear that, although the wind was high, they were to remain under steam. The constant racket and coal dust were a trial, necessitating a shampoo before dinner.

By the time the Tibaults and their guests assembled for dinner, the tension in the air was as palpable as the smell of soot. As usual, candlelight sparkled on the silver and crystal, and the table was set with yet another china pattern, more beautiful than the night before. As the steward turned her swivel chair in toward the table, Abigail needed no special powers of observation to note that Malcolm Tibault was holding himself aloof. Standing, as did the other gentlemen until all the ladies were in place, he was clearly in no humor to brook any questions regarding his decision to leave. Or the necessity for the unseemly speed. His demeanor as he unfolded his napkin, given her suspicions, made her nervous, an unaccustomed, and most uncomfortable feeling. She was not even tempted to try and lighten his humor, although it had been drilled into her that it was a guest's duty to try especially hard to be engaging when one's host appeared in need of cheering. Mercifully, Miss Donner would have no way of discovering her dereliction. Truth be told, she thought the resemblance between Malcolm Tibault and the gentleman so sorely in need of a tutor in *Le Bourgeois*

Gentilhomme was too close for comfort, and she dared not discuss the play with him for fear of letting something slip. In any case, he had launched on his favorite topic of the gold standard yet again, which she found as boring as baseball.

Although Ariadne tended to her hostess's duties with punctiliousness, setting the stewards to passing the tureen and serving the first wine, she also seemed strangely subdued. She left the delicious turtle soup untouched, and Abigail wondered if a quarrel with her husband might have precipitated her poor appetite. Certainly, if she had somehow found out about Emily's condition and suspected her husband's part in the matter, that would be cause enough for a row.

But it was not only the Tibaults who seemed distracted, even Peter and Jeramy seemed out of sorts. Jeramy had been quite the raconteur, amusing the entire table with tales of his exploits under water, until this evening. Surely he had nothing to do with Emily's predicament. Was there something else amiss? Glancing at Winifred, Abigail could even imagine that she seemed, well, preoccupied.

The captain had remained on the bridge, and Dr. Pettigrew had been detained in his surgery tending a clumsy stoker who'd managed to set his trousers alight with a hot coal.

Abigail sighed and glanced at Maude. No surcease from the gloom in that quarter. Maude had barely been civil as they had dressed for dinner. If the essence of yachting was to give pleasure, this cruise had suddenly turned into a dismal failure and was scarcely half done in spite of the steam. But why? Surely Emily's condition, while certainly a nuisance, was not of itself a weighty enough cause. Only the Houdinis seemed to still be enjoying themselves.

The after-dinner entertainment in the salon began awkwardly as well. Malcolm Tibault excused himself from the evening's festivities altogether, pleading unfinished tasks in light of their change in plans. Mrs. Tibault would remain as hostess. But it might have been better had she also excused herself. Seated in the chair most favorably placed to watch the magician's performance, she looked much like a castaway doll and only served to dampen the evening. Not even Houdini's magic with cards could coax a smile. At length, she did retire, and when Peter and Jeramy said their good nights, that left Abigail, Maude, and the Houdinis in the salon.

Abigail had no desire whatever to be confined alone in her stateroom with Maude until she was a good deal sleepier, and decided to take advantage of the opportunity of having two chaperons to finally ask the magician the question that had been bothering her since their first night out.

"I pray you, sir," she said as he settled down next to her on the curved settee after seating his wife and Maude in chairs facing them. "How did it come to pass that you knew I did not care to use a gun?"

"And would you use a firearm should the occasion arise?" he asked with a penetrating gaze.

"Never again." With a dark glance at Maude, she straightened her skirts so that they fell most becomingly. "I would very much like to know who told you."

Houdini smiled. "Then you do not believe I am psychic?"

"Mrs. Houdini told me how you worked the thought-reading trick."

"Giving away all my secrets, my love?" He glared at his wife with a mock serious frown. "If you continue thus, I shall not be able to make a living."

"Miss Danforth was much too clever, my dear," she replied with a grin. "She guessed."

Ordinarily Abigail would have taken umbrage at the accusation that she had guessed instead of deducing an answer through logic. But in this case, the magician's wife was accurate enough in her use of the word, and she let it pass. "How many of your . . . ah . . . tricks, or shall I say, how much of the magic you perform depends upon having a conspirator?" she asked.

"Almost all, Miss Danforth," he replied easily. "Perhaps you would be easier in your mind about what I do if you considered me an illusionist."

Abigail was astonished. Not so much by the answer, but that he would admit to it. She felt a grudging admiration for his candor and, unfurling her fan, fluttered it delicately.

"I amaze and mystify," he said dramatically. "Only to amuse," he added with a winning smile. "No harm done."

"Then might I ask how one of your more famous illusions is done?" Maude asked. "For the life of me I cannot imagine how you do it unless there is magic of some kind involved."

"It rather depends upon which illusion you are referring to, Miss Cunningham."

"How do you disappear from your horse?" she asked. "You vanish into thin air. There is absolutely no place for you to go. I would dearly love to know how you do it," she said, leaning forward eagerly.

"It is actually quite simple," Houdini replied with a shrug. "I disappear by becoming obvious."

"I beg your pardon?" Maude was utterly mystified.

"I will wager he has somehow taken a page from *The Purloined Letter*, Miss Cunningham," Abigail replied.

"Exactly so," he exclaimed.

"What on earth are you two talking about?" Maude asked. "What has a story by Poe to do with Houdini's disappearing from a horse in full view of an audience, pray tell?"

"I hide in plain sight," Houdini replied.

"But how?" Maude asked, losing patience.

"I am led on stage by my attendants who are all dressed in white. As I sit upon the horse, I am dressed in blue. My suit is made of paper." Holding out his hand toward Abigail to indicate that she should supply the answer, he added, "Need I say more, Miss Danforth?"

"How many attendants are there?" Abigail asked.

"Precisely," he exclaimed.

Exasperated, Maude shook her head. "I fail to understand what you two are talking about," she said, casting a glance at Mrs. Houdini, who shrugged and waited to hear what Abigail would say.

"I would wager that under Mr. Houdini's paper costume,

he is dressed like an attendant," Abigail said after thinking a moment. "When he is hidden from the audience by the cloth held high by more attendants, he tears off the suit, jumps off his horse, and, placing a cap upon his head, mingles with the attendants on stage."

Maude is amazed. "Has no one ever thought of counting the number of attendants?"

"Did you count them, Miss Cunningham?" Mrs. Houdini asked.

Maude blushed. "Well, no, I guess not," she replied, fanning herself briskly.

"I fear my husband is not being fair to himself, dear ladies," Mrs. Houdini said with an adoring glance at her husband. "Most of his illusions are really quite dangerous, requiring much practice and dexterity on his part."

"Not so," the magician exclaimed. "While they are designed to appear death defying, I would be foolish to perform them if I thought I would kill myself."

"But how do you escape when you are handcuffed, placed in a box that is shackled, and lowered into water?" Maude asked. "Is that not magic?"

"Not if he has a key about his person," Abigail said with an arched brow and sly smile.

"But he is searched by an entire committee," Maude protested.

"Did he not tell us he always works with a cohort?" Abigail replied. "He could easily pass this sleight-of-hand artist a key." She turned to Houdini. "Am I not right?"

"I am very glad you are not in the audience, Miss Danforth," he replied with a smile. "I would have a very difficult time of it. I fear our Dr. Conan Doyle thinks I am psychic. I wish I could convince him that I am a mere mortal."

"A most extraordinary mortal, sir," Abigail said graciously. And to her surprise, she meant it. Not only was he most generous in sharing his expertise but he also seemed genuinely respectful of his wife, as though she were actually an equal. A mate, not a possession. "But pray do not take your leave without telling me how you found out about my distaste for firearms."

"Since I have told you all of my secrets, I will save that one for myself, Miss Danforth." Standing, he held his hand out to his wife. "Come, my dear, we have packing to do if we are to disembark in the morning." As she stood by his side, he said, "I must confess I am not sorry to be leaving *The Seascape*, although I hasten to add that it has been a great pleasure getting to know you, Miss Danforth." Taking her extended hand, he kissed her fingertips in farewell. "And you, Miss Cunningham," he continued, bestowing upon her the same parting gesture. "There is too much unhappiness on board for my taste."

Maude gained her feet to leave, as did Abigail, who said with a wry smile, "Or can it be that happiness is merely an illusion?"

Abigail had hoped that *The Seascape* would remain in port long enough to attend the Houdinis' first performance, but it was not to be. Malcolm was adamant and, except for lingering dockside long enough to lay in more coal, they were under way again.

They had been at sea for most of the afternoon when the weather turned foul and showers forced everyone in. The strain between Abigail and Maude had not improved, and having no desire to keep company with her companion only to quarrel and always glad of the opportunity to read, Abigail discovered that she was without a book. Remembering Malcolm's well-stocked study and, after a few minutes' reflection which deck it was on, she decided to pay it a visit with Jacqueline in tow as chaperon. She had no trouble finding her way, and after knocking twice without hearing an answer, she tried the door. It was locked. There was nothing for it but to search for Malcolm Tibault.

But he was nowhere to be found. Peter, when located in the forward salon, had no key, nor did the captain. At last, they found Ariadne having her hair washed by Emily who, upon being interrupted, pointed at the tangle of keys on the dressing table and bade Abigail take them. Promising to return them forthwith, they repaired to the study once again. The second key worked, and it was with great relief that Abigail finally opened the door. Her pleasure was short-lived.

The once magnificent room was in shambles. One chair overturned, another shoved from its rightful place. Books torn from their shelves lay every which way on the carpet, and it looked as if an arm had swept across the top of his desk in a giant arc, dashing the contents helter skelter. The inkwell had shattered against the paneled wall from the force, blotching the precious wood and indelibly staining whatever it splashed. Blood-streaked vomit was everywhere.

Eyes wide, mouth agape, the horribly convulsed body of Malcolm Tibault sprawled, face up, on the carpet, a drool of blood-stained spittle congealed on his chin, his trousers stained at the crotch. It had not been an easy death.

▽

9

JACQUELINE SCREAMED.

Abigail stood at the threshold, staring at the grisly tableau. Upon hearing Jacqueline gather breath to scream again, she glared at her maid. "Scream again, and I shall be forced to slap you," she said coolly, before Jacqueline could let out another cry.

Stunned by her mistress's words and awed by her calm demeanor, Jacqueline swallowed hard and struggled to regain her composure.

"Fetch Mrs. Tibault," Abigail said with a wave of her hand for Jacqueline to be gone.

Stiff with shock, Jacqueline could but stare at Abigail and cover her mouth with both hands to keep from crying out again.

"No, no!" Abigail touched Jacqueline on the arm to stop her from leaving, a wasted gesture since her maid was still rooted to the spot. "The shock might be too great. Fetch Mr. Tibault from the salon."

Slowly, Jacqueline lowered her hands. Her face drained of all color, she blinked several times in amazement as she watched Abigail actually start into the room.

Abigail had no sooner set foot in the study when she changed her mind yet again. "No, no!" she cried. Turning, she held out her hand toward her maid to forestall her departure. "Fetch Captain Perkins. Tell him I need him on a matter most urgent." Holding her fingertips to her lips, "Pray, do not tell him the reason. No need to alarm the entire ship. Now hurry!"

Only too happy to escape the horrific sight, Jacqueline hurried away to do her mistress's bidding.

Abigail entered the study, closing the door behind her. A wall lamp cast its flickering light on the scene, as did a desk lantern. Mercifully, it had not been in the path of whatever had dashed the other contents of the desk onto the carpet, else the entire ship might now be in flames.

The odor of death was strong in the air, and Abigail pulled a handkerchief from the pocket of her voluminous skirts to breathe through. It seemed obvious that Malcolm had been poisoned, and since it was impossible to get close to his body without soiling her skirts, she sought to trace how he had done all the damage to the room by himself in his death throes.

If he had been seated behind his desk, he could have swept it clean when the first pains struck. Then he might have staggered across the room to tear the books from their shelves, stumbling into the chairs on his way. Or he might have been standing at the shelves when his ordeal began. But that would mean a trip over to get behind his desk to sweep it clear, and another back out to the middle of the floor. And why pull the books out at all? If he had the strength and time to destroy the room, why had he not simply yanked on the bellpull to summon help? Or run to the door? Suddenly aware of the bunch of keys in her hand, Abigail looked toward the door. No key in the lock. Had someone been in the room with him when he died? Had they fought? Since there was nothing for it but to examine his body for signs of violence other than the obvious contortions from expelling the poison, she placed the keys on the desk and, holding her handkerchief close to her nose, gathered her skirts to stoop down for a closer look. No sooner had she bent her knees than the light from the desk glinted on a golden object near his feet. Upon picking it up and turning it around, a chill of recognition struck her. It looked just like one of Maude's earrings.

* * *

Captain Perkins had no use for ladies on the bridge. When Miss Danforth, with her maid in tow, had sought him out looking for keys to Malcolm Tibault's study of all things, as if he were a steward, he had, however, been most patient and shown them every courtesy. The dark-eyed young beauty was a guest. And rumored to be wealthy. If there was anything that Thomas Perkins respected besides the sea, it was money, and the people who had a great deal of it.

His command of *The Seascape* capped a career more noted for its tribulations than triumphs. He signed on in spite of knowing Malcolm Tibault's reputation for being temperamental. In the event that he'd be summarily relieved of his post like so many of his predecessors, it would not be held against him when applying for another command since his part in the matter might be more believably excused. And he needed an easy berth to get his nerve back. His last command had been as captain of the ill-fated frigate, *Jezebel,* lost off the coast of Australia when she ran afoul of the Great Barrier Reef during a sudden squall. Half his crew perished, and he was considered lucky to have saved himself by holding on to a timber, which eventually washed ashore. To his everlasting shame, he'd not been the last to abandon ship. He'd known she was doomed before she hit, and there being no point in perishing for someone else's profit, he had not thought twice about saving himself when those sailors caught belowdecks did not turn to in time for the last lifeboat. Swamped by a wave, it, too, sank, and he fought to the death for that small piece of wood that kept him afloat. It was only after the investigation, when the survivors avoided looking at him square in the eye, that the doubts set in. He anticipated an easy time of it on *The Seascape.* Except for the vagaries of the sea itself, what could go wrong on a pleasure cruise? It had to be more leisurely than transporting cargo. It had to be safer than being at war.

Yet, there was a man overboard the day before they left Colon. The cavalier manner in which Malcolm smoothed over the incident with money impressed him, but left him troubled. And now this sudden mad dash for the States.

Under steam. The Caribbean was one of God's sweetest gifts to the seafarer, with waters from ink to palest green, and skies every color in the paint pot with fresh, balmy breezes aplenty. Possessed of a pretty, young wife, a yacht the likes of *The Seascape*, all the money he could ever need, why was Malcolm Tibault in such a hurry?

But it was not his place to question, only to obey. The chief engineer had assured him at length and vociferously that his engine was good for the run. An officer of the deck was on watch, and the rain had abated. Perkins was finally about to go below for a much needed rest when a breathless Jacqueline appeared in the doorway again. He was in no mood to be polite if not absolutely necessary, and not seeing her beautiful young mistress anywhere near, he allowed himself to sound as cross as he felt. "What are you doing here?" he demanded with a fearsome frown.

Already unnerved by the glimpse of Malcolm Tibault's body and further intimidated by the captain's forbidding visage, Jacqueline's English failed. "Oh, *Monsieur le Capitaine*," she said, her voice a breathless whisper. "I pray you . . . *Mlle*. Danforth, say . . . you must hurry."

"Hurry?" he asked impatiently. "Hurry where?"

Jacqueline had no words with which to give directions, and did her best to indicate the general location of Malcolm Tibault's study with her hands.

"Confound it," he exclaimed. "What is it you want from me?" He was annoyed by not understanding her waving hands, yet her body language had begun to amuse him. Waving his hands to mimic her, a grin formed at the corners of his mouth as he turned to the officer of the deck and navigator to see if they understood her any better.

Both shrugged, but neither man dared to smile just yet.

"Maybe you should follow her, sir," the navigator said respectfully. "She looks mighty upset."

"Oh, very well," he said. Turning to Jacqueline, he indicated with his hand that she should precede him from the bridge. "Show me the way."

And with that, Jacqueline was gone, apron strings flying. As fit as he was, Perkins was hard pressed to keep up with her as she fairly flew down the companionway and along the corridor to Malcolm Tibault's study. Reaching it first, it was Jacqueline who knocked on the closed door and, without waiting for an answer, opened it.

Abigail was stooped over Malcolm Tibault's body, and as Perkins stood in the threshold, all he could see was the destruction of the room. But there was no mistaking the smell. He entered the room, and as he drew close to her and identified the body at her feet, his thoughts raced ahead. With the owner dead, would *The Seascape* be sold? Would he be allowed to stay on as captain as part of the deal?

Abigail gained her feet and, handkerchief to her face, looked up at him.

Jacqueline remained by the door. Drawing out a handkerchief from her apron pocket, she held it over her nose and kept her eyes shut tight.

"Oh, my God, and sweet Jesus," Perkins said crossing himself. Removing his cap, he tucked it under his arm and, heading straight for the bellpull, gave it a hard yank.

His unannounced action made her forget the smell and Abigail lowered her hand. "What are you doing, pray tell?" she asked with alarm, tucking the handkerchief away in her skirts.

"Summoning a steward," he said, raking her with a glance that clearly bespoke his annoyance at her questioning him. "He must be buried at once."

"Oh, but you cannot," Abigail exclaimed. "I have not yet finished examining his body."

"I beg your pardon?" The captain could scarcely believe his ears. He was used to giving orders, and with one exception who lay dead at his feet, not taking them from anyone or having his actions questioned, certainly not by a mere snip of a girl. That she would wish to stay in the same room, alone, with a dead body much less examine it closely was incomprehensible.

"I had only just noticed the scratch on his forehead when you burst in here," Abigail said heatedly, not the least impressed by his rank. To her, he represented an employee—a most knowledgeable one to be sure and one who carried great responsibilities on his shoulders—but certainly no one to kowtow to.

Taken aback by her lack of repentance, he frowned disapprovingly. "My dear Miss Danforth," he replied in his most patronizing tone. "We have just crossed the Tropic of Cancer at about ninety degrees longitude—"

"I beg *your* pardon?" Abigail interrupted him without a qualm.

Perkins was not used to being interrupted, and it brought him up short. Her commanding demeanor could only mean that she was used to getting her way, and that in turn must mean that she had enough money to satisfy her whims. When he continued after a slight cough, there was a subtle but unmistakable shift in his tone. "Ah, you might say we are in the middle of nowhere as far as landfall is concerned, Miss Danforth." He shrugged nonchalantly, and was careful to sound as if he were speaking to an equal. "I should hope you would agree with me that since it is evident that Mr. Tibault died from ingesting something poisonous, there is no need to pickle him to preserve the body for evidence. If your holding a handkerchief to your nose is any indication, you yourself are experiencing what will soon overtake the entire ship if we do not get rid of his body at once."

"And what about informing the others?" Abigail asked. "No one knows that he is dead except you and me." She waved in the direction of the door. "And Jacqueline."

She was right, of course. Taking a few steps to the desk, he stroked the whiskers on his chin thoughtfully, trying to come up with a plan.

"No one else knows, except perhaps for the murderer," Abigail said, staring down at the body.

"He has been poisoned, Miss Danforth," Perkins said, indicating the state of the room with a sweeping gesture of his hand. "Anyone can see that."

"Just so," Abigail replied primly. "But by whom?"

"By himself for all we know," he replied firmly. "There are too many things in this world that are unhealthy to eat. Was not Mrs. Tibault's maid laid low for most of the voyage with indigestion?"

Faintly surprised that he would mention the indelicate subject of the state of a servant's health and not wanting to be switched away from the subject at hand, Abigail ignored his digression. "But look at the room," she cried. "Why did he not summon help if it was an accident?"

"With all due respect, Miss Danforth," he said, bowing ever so slightly, "I do not have time to engage in an argument with you. It is imperative that I get rid of the body before it infects the entire ship. We must have a service before nightfall."

"But you cannot mean to just knock on Mrs. Tibault's door and ask her to attend her husband's funeral," Abigail said, appalled by his callousness. "What about telling his son, for that matter?"

Perkins groaned and rubbed his beard again. She was right, of course. He'd been so focused on persuading her of the necessity of getting rid of the body immediately, that the ramifications of Tibault's death had escaped him for the moment. "Since you are a lady, it would be most kind of you, and I would be in your debt, if you would inform Mrs. Tibault, Miss Danforth. I will tell her son."

"Why do we not just assemble everyone in the main salon, and tell them all at once?" Abigail asked reasonably enough. Actually, she was eager to witness everyone's reaction when they heard the news.

Perkins shook his head. "The moment the stewards remove the body, the news will travel like lightning down a mast."

"I suppose you are right," she said slowly, having second thoughts. "Besides, asking everyone to gather would be cruel, would it not? They would no doubt think they were being invited to a party."

"Then you agree," he said with some relief. "Better they hear it from us privately."

"Us?" Abigail cast a swift glance at the anxious captain and sank onto the chair that was still in place. This was too good to be true. Especially in cases of poison it was most likely that the spouse was involved. It would provide her with a great advantage in solving the mystery if she could be the one to break the news to his wife and watch her reactions closely. Misunderstanding Abigail's silence for reluctance, Perkins turned on the charm. "You being a young lady and all, it would be kinder if you would tell his wife, do you not agree?" he asked pleasantly. Under the circumstances, he felt a smile would be out of place.

Abigail sighed heavily. "I suppose so," she replied as if bestowing a large favor.

"I will break it to his son and the other guests."

"And Miss Dupree?" Abigail asked, concealing her eagerness to have the assignment of telling her as well.

"Oh, how kind of you, Miss Danforth," Perkins said, much relieved, assuming that her question meant that she was volunteering. "You would be so much better than I with the fair sex," he continued, somewhat distractedly. He was trying to remember where he had stowed a black armband even though he had only stopped wearing one when he had joined *The Seascape*. And had he packed a Bible in his gear? Or at the least a book of common prayer? He was about to have a look at the books strewn about, when there was a knock at the door.

Jacqueline looked at him expectantly and, with a curt nod, he gave his permission to open it.

The steward gasped when he beheld the grisly scene, and for one awful moment Abigail thought he might faint.

"Fetch Dr. Pettigrew, and bring me some tarp for the body, son," Perkins demanded. "And have a couple buddies with you—enough to carry the body."

Open-mouthed, the steward turned away to obey.

"Oh, and while you are about it," Perkins added, when he had the steward's attention, "have someone inform Mr. Tibault's valet, or you do it if you know him well enough.

Then send someone below to find a plank. Tell him to place it near the railing abaft the funnel on the port side."

As Jacqueline let the steward out, Perkins consulted his watch. "Do tell the ladies that I shall expect them there at four bells . . . ah . . . in about an hour."

"Only one hour, sir?" Abigail protested, moving to the desk to retrieve the keys. "His wife might not have recovered her wits in that short time. She is only a young girl."

"Very well," he said. "But if she is not there by six o'clock, over he goes without her."

By the time Abigail and Jacqueline reached the companion-way, Abigail realized that she and Maude would need something to wear to the funeral, if one could call it that, and dismissed Jacqueline to dig out her black gown from the trunk in storage. Failing that in the short time available, she was to find a suitable hat. And find the same for Maude as well as for herself.

As Jacqueline dashed off to do her bidding, Abigail hurried toward the cabin she shared with Maude for the smelling salts. She refused to carry it on her person as most girls did, but if Ariadne were to need it, she wished to be prepared.

She had no idea where Maude was, and was in a quandary whether to search for her before informing Ariadne of her widowhood. But when she discovered Maude in their stateroom, although she was determined not to mention the earring reposing in her pocket until she checked Maude's collection for the mate, she felt she had little choice but to tell her what had happened.

"Well, I for one am not surprised," Maude said in response to the news.

Flabbergasted by her companion's reaction, Abigail was loath to leave. But there was too much to do in too little time to begin a discussion that threatened to take hours. Locating the smelling salts in the dressing table drawer, she grabbed it and fled the room.

* * *

Ariadne scarcely reacted to the news of her widowhood, which Abigail attributed to shock. However, Emily, who was putting the finishing touches to her mistress's hair, fainted dead away.

Abigail eventually located Winifred Dupree in her stateroom, readying herself for tea. Except for growing quite pale, she remained remarkably calm upon hearing the news. She had a dozen questions, of course, but understood when Abigail begged off answering them until afterward. She readily agreed to meet with everyone topside.

Captain Perkins found Peter lounging in the forward salon with Jeramy, drinks in hand. Drawing close, he removed his cap and tucked it under his arm. "I do not know how to break this to you, son," he said solemnly.

Peter glanced at Jeramy before turning his attention to Perkins. "Oh?"

Perkins suddenly realized that the young man who stared back at him might soon become the owner of the yacht, and he was just as suddenly tongue-tied. "Your father is . . . ah . . . how shall I say . . . ah . . . this is awkward," he stammered, seating himself in a nearby chair.

Again, Peter and Jeramy exchanged glances before looking at the captain.

"Miss Danforth has just found your father's body," Perkins continued lamely.

"His body?" Peter said, placing his drink on the table. "What do you mean, his body? Is he dead?"

"I am afraid that is about the size of it, son," Perkins said. "My men are just now sewing him into a shroud. We must have a service quite soon."

"But can I not see him?" Peter got to his feet.

Perkins shook his head. "Better not, son," he replied, standing also. "It was not a pretty sight."

"But what happened?" Peter asked. "How did he die?"

"I do not mean to leave you with so many unanswered

questions, Mr. Tibault," Perkins replied, donning his cap. "But I must excuse myself, I have much to do before the . . . ah . . . ceremony." Pulling his watch from his pocket, he said, "In somewhat more than an hour from now. We can talk at length, afterward."

Accompanied by drumrolls of distant thunder, dark clouds gathered overhead as the black-clad widow, his son, guests of *The Seascape*, the captain, servants, and selected sailors surrounded a plank teetering on the railing that held Malcolm Tibault's weighted, shrouded body.

Captain Perkins had just finished the Lord's Prayer, and was about to order the sailors to tip the plank when Peter cried out, "How do I know that it is my father in there?"

With a silent nod at the sailors standing at the head of the plank, Perkins granted his permission for Peter to have a last look.

As one sailor held the board solid, the other pulled a knife from his pocket, sliced open the tarpaulin, and pulled it down far enough for Peter to get a look at the body's face.

Peter shuddered, and had it not been for Jeramy standing near, he might have collapsed.

Another signal from the captain, and the sailors tilted the plank. With a distinctive, rasping sound that Abigail would not soon forget, Malcolm Tibault's body was committed to the deep.

▽

10

As if the body entering the sea were a cue for the heavens to weep, it began to rain in earnest. The servants and those sailors not on watch made an unceremonious dash forward to the port-side stairwell leading to their quarters. The rest of the mourners scurried into the forward deckhouse, the gentlemen hanging back to allow the ladies to enter first.

Missing were the giggles and pleasantries that would have ordinarily accompanied such an unceremonious run for cover, but there was much rustling of petticoats as the ladies took a moment to shake their skirts before taking the arm of an escort. Thence they proceeded two-by-two, with proper decorum befitting the tragedy, toward the companionway that led to the salon belowdecks.

Captain Perkins led the way with Ariadne on his arm and, realizing it would be brief and desiring to make the most of their proximity, offered his condolences. "And with your permission," he added, "I shall set sail as soon as the storm abates."

Close behind them, Peter could not help but overhear this last remark, and the captain's assumption that the widow should be the one to authorize any changes in his father's orders unsettled his already shaky composure. Did the man somehow know the yacht would be hers? Excusing himself from Winifred, he stepped forward to confront him. "Better you ask for my permission," he said with a menacing frown. "*The Seascape* is mine now."

"Pay him no mind." Ariadne clung tightly to the captain's

arm. "His father disinherited him some time ago, poor boy." Her voice was so muffled by her heavy veil that Perkins had to bend down to hear her over the drone of the engine as she continued. "I would be most grateful if you did switch to sail, sir. I confess I am weary of all the noise and smut."

Peter stood his ground, and was about to protest further when Winifred pulled on his sleeve and motioned for him to allow them to move on. He looked at her with annoyance, but a quick glance past her at the others who had been forced to stop at the head of the stairs, convinced him she was right. Time enough to set the captain straight when they reached the salon.

But as soon as they entered the paneled room, Ariadne asked that the gentlemen move three chairs to face the built-in double settee so that they would form a conversational circle, while the salon steward rearranged the side tables. By the time Peter had finished helping Winifred and Maude settle themselves on the settees, the captain and Amos Pettigrew had moved to the far side of the room, and were about to lift two overstuffed chairs to comply with Ariadne's wishes. Having no desire to air his grievance in public, and there being no further chairs to be moved, Peter went over to the piano to stay out of the way of the commotion. As he turned to face the room, Jeramy sidled up to him. "When are you going to order him to turn about?" he whispered, casting a meaningful glance at the captain.

"Turn her about?" Peter also kept his voice low since he was no longer so certain that he had the right to command the captain to do anything. "Whatever for?"

Jeramy drew back and looked at Peter as if he were a simpleton. "To dive for the empress's snuff boxes," he said with a worried frown.

"What do I need snuff boxes for now?" Peter asked haughtily. "I shall soon be in possession of my father's fortune."

"What if he left everything to her?" Jeramy glanced over his shoulder at Ariadne, who had settled herself in one of the chairs.

"In a pig's eye," Peter scoffed. "You heard him."

"But that does not mean he left anything to you," Jeramy said. "He could have donated it all to charity."

"Charity?" Peter drew his lips down in a scornful smirk. "My father's only charity was himself. I am his only son," he continued with a lift to his chin, his tone belligerent. "I am his rightful heir." Even as he spoke, Peter doubted his words, and before Jeramy could question him further, he turned away and left to join the circle.

As Jeramy moved away from the piano, he almost bumped into the second salon steward who had entered the nearby doorway carrying a tray of artfully arranged sandwiches and delicacies. The first salon steward, having completed his chore of arranging the tables, looked about the room for Peter. Locating him in the chair nearest Winifred on the settee, he showed him the label on the bottle of wine he proposed to serve. Peter nodded his approval, and with a flick of his fingers that exactly mimicked his father's gesture, signaled that he should open it.

Abigail was more than a little surprised that the young widow had arranged for refreshments to follow so hard upon the brief service. She might be hostessing a lawn party instead of burying a husband. Tea had been missed, and dinner was to be forsworn, so the repast was welcome. But for a girl of her tender years to exhibit such thoughtfulness in the face of her recent loss almost exceeded the bounds of good taste. Perhaps she was in shock. Or suspect? Certainly, Emily had produced widow's weeds in a trice. Had the widow been prepared for her widowhood? Or had Jacqueline worked her magic again? Her maid had, after all, found two black gowns in Maude's trunks. Perhaps she had found a third in her own, since she and Ariadne were almost the same size. In any case, it was only Winifred who had been unable to come up with anything but a somber blue linen suit on such short notice. Every hat that graced a lady's head, however, was unadorned black straw, swathed in black netting, which each had set about untying and rearranging, the better to dry out, the moment they seated themselves.

Both Pettigrew and Peter were in proper black, with armbands, but Jeramy had had to make do with navy flannel.

Captain Perkins, of course, had remained in uniform, with armband. The last to seat himself, he no sooner took a chair next to Ariadne's when, after approving the wine, Peter cleared his throat. "What, precisely, happened to my father?" he asked.

Both stewards, eager to hear every word, acted as if they were not listening as they continued to serve.

Although Peter was looking at Captain Perkins when he spoke, clearly intending for him to be the one to respond, it was Amos Pettigrew who spoke. "I do not know that we can be precise, Mr. Tibault," he replied, shooting a swift glance at Perkins.

"Agreed," the captain said with a decisive nod. "All we can say, for certain, is that he ingested enough of something poisonous to kill him."

"But what could that be?" Peter asked. "He was perfectly healthy this morning."

"It could have been any number of things," Amos said with a shrug. "Bad seafood comes to mind—"

"We have all partaken of the same food, have we not?" Peter interrupted. "Why have we not been stricken?"

Winifred shuddered and swiftly withdrew her hand from a beautifully decorated, but unidentifiable, morsel on the tray.

The surgeon shrugged, and with a glance at the captain for corroboration, said, "I cannot answer that, son."

Although she had promised herself to keep silent until she had heard all the facts, Abigail could not bear this glossing over of details. "Had you not ordered the room scoured and tidied, you might have gotten a sample of what had been in his stomach and shown it to the authorities in New Orleans," she said sarcastically.

"I do not need anyone to tell me how to run a tight ship, Miss Danforth," Perkins replied, his face red in an effort to control his temper at being challenged by this snippet of a girl. "There was no cup or glass about—"

"Are we still bound for the States?" Jeramy interrupted with exaggerated innocence. Glancing at Peter, he continued, "That is to say, it is your ship, is it not? We could just as easily return to Martinique."

Peter glared at him in silence.

"But it has all the earmarks of strychnine poisoning," Abigail protested, annoyed that the conversation had veered off the subject. "The way his body was contorted, his grimace—"

Prefacing her remark with a tsking sound, Maude shook her head disapprovingly. "How like you to think of murder, Miss Danforth."

"Murder!" Ariadne exclaimed. Unfurling her fan with a snap, she fluttered it violently.

"The poison is commonly used to exterminate rats," Abigail continued. "I should think there would be an abundant supply on board."

"Rats?" Winifred shuddered, fluttering her fan vigorously. "Ugh!"

"The room was in shambles," Abigail continued firmly.

Before she could continue, Perkins broke in, "All of which could be ascribed to the death throes, Miss Danforth."

"But why did he not ring for help?" Abigail asked. "Or open the door and cry out? He certainly had time to do so if he had time to throw all those books on the floor."

"She is right, you know," Pettigrew said, leaning forward for a better view of the captain.

"But who would want my father dead?" Peter glared directly at Jeramy as he spoke.

With Maude's earring all but burning a hole in her pocket, Abigail decided it was better not to speculate.

"Do not look at me," Jeramy exclaimed, eyes wide with horror. "I only want to turn back to Martinique. Apparently we are not going to do so."

"Oh, I pray you, let us not turn back," Maude said earnestly.

Abigail looked at her in astonishment.

"Hear! Hear!" Pettigrew seconded.

"I, too, insist that we continue on our course," Ariadne said. "My husband's lawyers reside in New Orleans."

"Hah!" Peter exclaimed. "And you think you are in his will?"

"And you do not?" she cried.

"Why would you be in his will?" Peter said scornfully. "He was going to divorce you."

The stewards froze. Divorce was unheard of, and certainly not a subject to be mentioned in polite company.

Maude gasped.

Winifred paled.

The captain and Pettigrew both gazed at their shoes in an agony of embarrassment.

Open-mouthed, Abigail stared first at Peter, then at Ariadne. The threat of divorce would certainly be motive enough for murder.

Outraged, Ariadne stood. "How could you say such a thing!" she cried.

All the gentlemen, including Peter, were on their feet in an instant.

"Tell her, Mr. Singleton," Peter said defiantly. "You were there when he said it."

"He is telling the truth, Mrs. Tibault," Jeramy replied solemnly, concealing his glee at this turn of events.

Ariadne clapped her hands to her ears and, collapsing into her chair, began to sob.

Much to her dismay, Abigail realized she preferred to think Ariadne guilty of murder rather than Maude, no matter the evidence.

"Now look what you have done," Winifred cried. In one smooth motion, she rose and then knelt by Ariadne's chair, pulling smelling salts from her reticule.

"Enough!" Captain Perkins's voice cut through the weeping and muttering. "As long as we are on the high seas, my word is law. And I say we continue to New Orleans. *The Seascape* is registered there. And if Mr. Tibault's lawyers are there, so much the better. Now if you will excuse me." With a shallow bow, he turned on his heel to take his leave.

"Captain Perkins," Abigail called out. The captain stopped, but when he turned to look at her it was with a frown on his face that said he would brook no nonsense. Unperturbed by his fierce demeanor, she said coolly, "About how long will it take to reach land?"

"A day and a half, two at most, Miss Danforth," he replied briskly. "That is, if I have no interference."

Not to be fobbed off so easily, Abigail continued. "And you and Dr. Pettigrew agree that Mr. Tibault's death was due to an accidental ingestion of tainted fish?"

"Oh, come, come, Miss Danforth," Maude exclaimed. "Your morbid thirst for adventure is most assuredly misplaced in this instance." Indicating the people in the room with a gracious sweep of her hand, she said, "Who among these lovely people had motive, pray tell? Even his son and widow are unsure about their inheritances. Both the captain and Dr. Pettigrew stand to lose their positions should *The Seascape* be sold. For whatever reason Mr. Singleton wishes to return to Martinique, it is apparently doing him no good to have Mr. Tibault dead."

The drone of the engine was palpable in the silence that followed Maude's outburst as the captain's piercing gaze swept the room before reaching Pettigrew, who gave an almost imperceptible nod of assent. "I think I speak for all of us aboard, Miss Danforth, when I tell you that it is best that you do not meddle." And with that, he was gone.

Utterly distraught, Emily refused to take part in the repast in the servants' mess, and fled immediately to the cabin she shared with Jacqueline.

Jacqueline had seldom been so tired. She had not stopped running, from the moment she had accompanied her mistress to find the keys to the study until she had stood still to listen to the captain's last words. Immensely grateful to finally be sitting at a well-set table, her hand trembled as she reached for her glass of wine. In light of her extended service during the endless afternoon, Abigail gave her the night off. A long evening loomed ahead, and she most sincerely hoped that Emily would recover herself sufficiently to resume her duties so that she could enjoy it, and have the cabin to herself for a while.

Both Boris and Carlotta were in shock, but that did not keep Boris from bombarding Jacqueline with questions while Carlotta sat next to him, horrified by the tiny maid's responses. When, at length, the sandwiches were passed, Jacqueline discovered that she had no appetite. She did, however, accept another glass of wine.

Furious with Maude for embarrassing her in front of the captain in the salon, and preoccupied with her thoughts, Abigail said not a word to her the rest of the evening. Nor did she speak even when they had finally returned to their stateroom and she was readying herself for bed. But anyone watching her could not help but notice her state of mind. Normally neat when Jacqueline was not on duty, she yanked at her hat pins and flung her clothes to land where they would over the chair. By the time she transferred the incriminating earring to the pocket of her dressing gown, the only reason she could come up with for such a betrayal was that Maude had need of protecting herself.

Maude waited until Abigail was seated at the dressing table, took her hair down, and began brushing it. Strolling casually over to the birdcage, she glanced in Abigail's direction. "Well?" she said, a bemused expression on her face.

"Well, what," Abigail snapped.

"Do not feign innocence with me, Miss Danforth," Maude responded calmly. "A stranger could see that you are angry. And I am no stranger."

Abigail could not resist Maude's invitation. "How dare you undermine me in front of all of those people," she cried. "You sounded just like Dr. Conan Doyle. I felt an absolute fool."

"When you have quite finished your pet, I shall tell you," Maude replied, quitting the birdcage to stroll to her bed and sit on the side.

"I am not in a pet," Abigail exclaimed, the heat in her tone belying her words.

"If you were not so angry with me right now you might see what I was trying to do."

The brush caught a snarl, and rather than respond Abigail concentrated on loosening the tangle.

"Perhaps you are right after all, Miss Danforth," Maude said. "Emotions do not belong in an investigation. Certainly not anger."

"You know I cannot bear conundrums, Miss Cunningham. Get to the point!"

"Is it true that you suspect skulduggery in the matter of Mr. Tibault's death?"

"Well, yes, of course—"

Maude held out a forestalling hand. "If you are indeed sincere and if your premise is true, then the killer probably thinks he or she has gotten away with it, is this not so?"

Abigail rolled her eyes heavenward in exasperation at the obvious.

"You are still so upset—dare I say emotional?—you cannot see," Maude exclaimed with a sardonic smile.

If indeed a murder had been committed, Ariadne naturally would have been Abigail's prime suspect. Thus Abigail wondered if she should put their friendship to the test by showing her the earring since it would necessarily imply that she suspected Maude. But now her patience was at an end, and, still holding the brush in one hand, she reached into her pocket with the other and, pulling out the earring, dangled it in the air.

"Where did you find that?" Maude rose from the edge of the bed, and took the few steps to reach Abigail.

"In Malcolm Tibault's study," Abigail replied, looking Maude in the eye. "Is it yours?"

Blushing, Maude held out her hand.

Her face grim, Abigail dropped the earring into Maude's outstretched palm and began brushing her hair again.

Maude looked at her in wonderment. "You cannot mean that you suspect me?"

"I have no wish to suspect you of murder, Miss Cunningham. However, you were obviously in his study. Probably with Mr. Tibault. Alone."

Maude strolled over to the birdcage. "Yes, that is true," she replied sheepishly. "But that certainly does not mean I killed him." She paused and looked at Abigail directly. "I might have wanted to, but even that does not mean that I poisoned him."

"Why would you wish to kill him, pray?" Abigail asked, amazed by her admission.

"I do not wish to go into that now, if you please," Maude said with a heavy sigh. "However, it is beginning to appear to me that the men I care for die."

Struck by the genuine grief in Maude's voice, Abigail slowly placed the brush on the table and started to get up.

Maude held out a hand, warning her to keep her distance. "Little did I know that you suspected me when I made my remarks."

Realizing that Maude had every right to be angry, Abigail sat back down and began to braid her hair as if she had not made the gesture toward comforting her friend. "And pray tell, why did you?" she said, but there was no longer any heat in her tone, merely curiosity.

"Did it not occur to you that the killer was in the room and might come after you if you made it public that you intended to catch him?" Before Abigail could speak, she swiftly added, "Or her?"

Abigail stared at Maude, her hands stilled. Maude was right. She had been so intent upon the puzzle, it had not occurred to her that she'd be in any danger.

Abigail's expression was all the validation that Maude required. "If you intend to persist, my dear, I should warn you to watch what you eat with the greatest of care."

"But I cannot just let a killer go free," Abigail cried.

Maude paused before saying, ever so gently, "Even if you proved that it was I who poisoned him?"

Abigail stood. "Miss Cunningham!" Now that Maude had expressed her worst fears, she wanted nothing more than to ask Maude's forgiveness for being so suspicious.

Maude forestalled Abigail's impending apology with a shrug. "Now it is I who insist that you satisfy yourself that Mr. Tibault's death was an accident. Or if it was murder, to unmask the killer if you can," she said, her voice firm. "If nothing else, it would serve to clear my name in your mind."

"I shall do what I can, Miss Cunningham," Abigail replied solemnly. "We have not got much time."

Suddenly aware she'd been maneuvered into encouraging the young detective against her better judgment, Maude shook her head. "Take care," she said, trying to keep the worry from her tone.

▽

11

Whewhen the ship shuddered and lurched to starboard, it caught Ariadne off guard. She stumbled but managed to gain her balance by grabbing the back of her dressing-room chair. Although the racket of the engine stopped, and only the normal creak and groan of timbers could be heard as *The Seascape* made way under sail once again, it did little to improve her humor. She turned to glare at Emily who had finally appeared in the doorway. "It is about time you got here," she said crossly.

"Sorry, miss." She, too, had almost fallen when the ship changed position underfoot, but knew better than to try and use her unsteady footing as an excuse.

"Do not apologize again, for heaven's sake," Ariadne replied. "I am fairly sick with your apologizing all the time."

"Beg pardon, miss." Emily clapped a hand to her mouth. The words had escaped before she realized what she was saying.

"Enough, I say." Beside herself with frustration, Ariadne's voice rose. "Just try not to be so slow when I ring for you." Turning her back to Emily, she said, "Now undo me."

Worried about her fate now that Tibault was dead, completely discombobulated by her near fall, and her mistress's temper, Emily could scarcely find the back of Ariadne's dress, much less the buttons.

"What is the matter with you," Ariadne exclaimed impatiently when Emily fumbled.

Emily grabbed a handkerchief from her apron pocket, and blew her nose.

Ariadne turned to face her obviously distressed maid. "Oh, I might as well give you something to cry about since you seem so intent upon it," she said scornfully.

Stunned, Emily swiftly wadded her handkerchief, and jammed it back into the pocket.

"As soon as we land you are to leave this ship." Ariadne's voice was cold as ice. "You will no longer be in my employ."

Emily gasped. "He told you?"

Ariadne's eyes narrowed with suspicion. "Did who tell me what?"

Realizing her mistake too late, Emily started to move around Ariadne to try with the buttons again. "Nothing, ma'am," she muttered.

"No." Ariadne circled with her so that Emily still faced her, and peered closely into her maid's face. "There was something there," she said, squinting. "I saw it. Tell me."

Emily ducked her head, and looked away from her mistress's piercing gaze.

Grabbing Emily by the shoulders, Ariadne shook her until her cap was askew. "Did you talk to my husband behind my back?" she shouted. Dropping her hands, she glared at her maid.

Although her mistress was much smaller, her demeanor was so fierce and her position so exalted that it did not occur to Emily to defend herself. Knowing she was guilty made her even more vulnerable. Near tears, she could not look up. "Never," she said, her voice scarcely above a whisper.

Sensing her maid was lying and desperate to know the truth, Ariadne slapped her across the face so hard her hand stung.

Emily cried out and put her hands to her face. "Oh, I pray thee ma'am, do not hit me no more," she said through her fingers. "It warn't my fault. He said it would be my job if I did not."

"Did not what?" Ariadne's voice was fierce.

Hands still to her face, Emily shook her head in shame.

Ariadne slapped her again.

Emily shrieked.

Already knowing what her maid's answer was going to be, Ariadne was nonetheless desperate to hear it. Knowing that if she hit Emily again, she would merely delay her response, she controlled the urge and forced herself to sit. When Emily calmed herself enough to hear, she put all the venom in her voice that she could muster and said, "I swear I shall have you dropped over the side if you do not tell me what my husband forced you to do."

Dabbing at her eyes with her handkerchief, Emily's voice was barely above a whisper. "To lie with him."

Even though she now knew the worst, Ariadne did not want to believe it. "You slept with my husband?" she cried.

"No, ma'am," Emily snuffled, and caught her breath. "We did not sleep none."

Ariadne struck the back of the chair with her hand. "You know what I mean!" she exclaimed impatiently.

Emily could but shake her head in response.

Turning to face the mirror, Ariadne looked into it as she asked, "Did you do this . . . did you lie with him before or after we were married?"

Emily groaned and put her hands to her face again.

Ariadne stood, lifting her hand as if to strike her.

Emily cringed and held out her hands to ward off the blow. "Both!" she cried.

Wild with fury, Ariadne slapped her again with all her might, then sank to the dressing-room chair, sobbing.

"Oh, I am so sorry, ma'am," Emily cried between sobs. "He made me do it. Honest I did not want to none."

"Oh shut up!" Ariadne shouted, opening the dressing-table drawer and groping for a handkerchief. "You are making it worse!" She slammed the drawer shut.

"I am sorry, ma'am." Overwhelmed by her predicament, Emily tried to control her tears.

Taking a deep breath, Ariadne tried to compose herself,

but then another thought struck her. "Oh, my God in heaven," she cried, turning in the chair to look at her maid, horrified. "You have not been seasick at all."

Emily cringed.

"I will wager you are with child!" she exclaimed. Gaining her feet she strode to the chaise. Turning, she faced Emily. "You are carrying my husband's baby." She stated it as a fact; there was no question whatever in her tone.

Emily hung her head in shame.

"Well, you must get rid of it at once," Ariadne said briskly, afraid that the baby might have some claim upon her already shaky inheritance.

"Beg pardon, ma'am." Emily stared at her blankly. "What do you mean?"

"Have Dr. Pettigrew do something," Ariadne replied impatiently.

"Do something?" Emily asked, bewildered. "What can he do?"

"You cannot give birth to my husband's bastard!" Ariadne shouted, striding toward her. "I will not allow it!"

Emily was horrified. "But I cannot kill my baby!" she cried.

"Oh, yes you can! And you will! Or I shall see that you leave this ship with nothing but the clothes on your back!" Ariadne shook her finger under Emily's nose, her tone menacing. "No money, and no references."

"Oh, ma'am, you cannot mean to be so cruel."

"Do not mistake me, girl," Ariadne replied, her eyes narrow. "I will not be so publicly humiliated."

"But I cannot kill my baby," Emily cried, wringing her hands.

"You have that baby aborted or else."

"But I would go straight to hell." Emily's voice was thin with terror. "I would burn forever and ever."

"It would serve you right for what you have done to me." Ariadne sat at the dressing table and began fishing for the pins in her hair. "Now get out of here."

Emily was immobilized by the impossible dilemma.

"Be gone, I say!" Ariadne turned in her chair and waved angrily at her maid. "I will undress myself. I cannot bear the sight of you."

As she stared at her mistress, Emily wondered how on earth her life had come to such a terrible pass when all she had ever done was to obey her betters. With a heavy, inconsolable sigh, she turned and, once again, went away as she was told.

Winifred made it through the funeral without crying. Peter had looked at the contorted face inside the shroud, but she did not go near it nor had she any desire to. The body inside could have been anyone, and although she understood it to be Malcolm Tibault's, she did not want to believe—nay, she could not believe—that he was actually dead.

She also made it through the wake, as well as the rest of the evening, without crying. True, Malcolm had not appeared, but there again, he frequently failed to show up at functions he was expected to attend, even some of those where he was host. More than once, it was because they were locked in an embrace in some hidden corner of his, or their host's, home, and occasionally in a shady cul-de-sac provided by some bushes in a garden. Brief as those encounters were, they were all the more exciting for being stolen, and their very swiftness kept her in thrall.

Since his first wife, Annabelle, had been prone to jealousy, she probably suspected something was going on between them, but since they were never caught, Winifred was fairly certain that Annabelle went to her grave without knowing the truth. Even had she found out, Winifred was not sure she could have stopped herself. She tried, countless times, but whenever he beckoned, his sleepy-eyed grin proved irresistible, and she succumbed anew. They had a terrible row, of course, when he took Ariadne to be his wife, but it was mostly show on her part. In her heart of hearts she did not want to be the one he cheated on but rather the one he cheated with.

Unable to resist him, she enjoyed her role as temptress. Now he was gone. Never again would he beckon to her.

Plumping the pillow, she turned her face into it, hoping that the tears she knew were there, would come. But instead, a pounding in her temples distracted her. And thus began a headache, the severity of which she had never before known.

Awake before first light, Abigail dressed herself in a black cotton frock and, with a severe twist to her hair, managed to pin it up so that, except for those tendrils that escaped at her ears, her hat of black straw hid its imperfections. Carlotta was much impressed when she appeared with her morning tea and toast. Jacqueline, who appeared shortly thereafter even though she had not been summoned, less so.

None of this activity disturbed Maude, who continued to sleep soundly, even after Abigail dismissed the servants and, ignoring the tea, set out for Dr. Pettigrew's surgery. She was much impressed with his professionalism in keeping Emily's secret. She hoped he would not be so close-mouthed when it came to discussing Malcolm Tibault's widow and son, but mostly she wished to have his professional opinion regarding the possibility of Mr. Tibault's having been poisoned. All the remarks about her morbid thirst for adventure to the contrary, she had no stomach for pursuing a murderer where there was none.

Accustomed to having men seek his services at any time, day or night, Amos Pettigrew seldom thought of running a comb through his hair, much less of brushing his teeth, before answering a knock on his door when the hour was odd. He was most discomfited when he opened his door and saw that it was Abigail, fully dressed, standing in the corridor. Assuming she must be in dire straits to seek him out at such an indecently early hour, and mildly curious about why she had not summoned him to her bedside instead of making the trip herself, he swiftly opened the door wide to let her in. As she stepped into his quarters, he glanced down the hall before closing the door to see who was accompanying her and was surprised to find that she was unchaperoned. Suddenly realizing how disheveled he was, he was much embarrassed and ran a hand through his hair. He was thankful that he'd at least put his feet into slippers and thrown a robe over his nightclothes. Tying the belt more securely about his waist, he asked, "Is there something the matter, Miss Danforth?"

Abigail thought she smelled stale whiskey on his breath. Or was the room simply permeated with alcohol? Surely no one had a drink before breakfast, least of all a doctor. "No, nothing is the matter with me," she replied. "But I have come to seek your good counsel, if you please."

"Can it not wait?" he asked, stifling a yawn.

"I do pray you excuse the hour, but there is little time left," she said with a winsome smile. "I have some questions of grave import, and you are the only one who can answer them."

"Then pray excuse *me*," he said. Not a little impressed with her determination, he headed for the door to his private quarters. "I shall dress at once. Do sit down," he said, indicating the chair beside his desk. "I will be but a moment."

Abigail remained standing, time enough to sit when he returned. The small outer office was curtained on one side, and a quick peek behind it revealed an examining table with an enamel side table for instruments. Behind his desk, which was clear except for the usual quill pen and inkpot, stood an enamel windowed supply cabinet filled with all manner of powders and potions in bottles that sat in holes in a tray, presumably so that they would not tip over when the motion of the ship became violent in heavy weather. Dozens of keys were on unmarked pegs inside as well. The creak and moan of the ship's timbers masked the sound of the door opening, and Abigail was startled to hear Pettigrew's voice. "Did Mr. Houdini activate an interest in keys, Miss Danforth?" Indicating that she should take the chair beside his desk, he strode to the chair in back of it. Once she had settled herself comfortably, he sat.

"You seem to have quite a collection, sir," she said, arranging her skirt to fall properly.

"I have all the keys to whatever has locks on *The Seascape* in case of an emergency, Miss Danforth."

"Mr. Tibault's study was locked," she said. "There was no key inside."

He shrugged.

Abigail glanced at the row of bells on the wall behind him, above the supply cabinet. "You can be summoned from many places on the ship, I see."

Again, he shrugged. "Also for emergencies."

"I gather Mr. Tibault did not ring for you?"

"Come, come, Miss Danforth, do not toy with me," he said with a frown. "Just what is it you are after?"

Abigail smiled sweetly, as if he had caught her in a game. "You saw that room before Mr. Tibault's body was taken away," she said, leaning close in a conspiratorial fashion.

Pettigrew gave her an appraising look, indicating that she should continue.

"What was your impression?" she asked. "What did you think?"

Pettigrew sighed heavily, wishing he could have a couple of fingers of brandy. "It seemed to me that he had a rough time dying."

"More than that?"

"I confess I did not analyze the room, Miss Danforth."

"Then did you see any marks on his body?"

"His face was contorted—"

"No, no," Abigail interrupted impatiently. "Did he look as if he might have been in a fight? I had just noticed that he had a scratch on his forehead when the captain appeared."

Pettigrew rubbed his chin as he looked at Abigail appraisingly. "The cause of death seemed so obvious that I confess I did not look too closely for other signs."

She leaned forward eagerly, her eyes agleam. "Do you really think it was tainted fish, sir?"

He shrugged. "It could have been."

"Could it not have been strychnine?"

"How do you know so much about poisons?"

"I had occasion to do some reading when I was in Honolulu."

"I must say I agree that your selection of reading material tends toward the morbid."

"Do you have anything else in your pharmacology that would have created such . . . ah . . . symptoms?"

"Miss Danforth," he exclaimed, and standing, he moved around his desk to stand over her. "Are you accusing me?"

Wondering how she could have possibly offended him, Abigail stared at him quizzically.

"I am the last person who would want to see Malcolm Tibault dead." He paced toward the curtain. "He was my bread and butter."

"But you can practice medicine anywhere."

Pettigrew swept his arm in a wide arc, indicating the entire ship. "In a style like this?"

"I did not mean to offend you." Abigail sighed. "I was merely trying to educate myself."

"You certainly are observant for a girl." His glance was speculative as he continued, "Or are you now playing at being a detective?"

Abigail ignored the jibe. "Except for the untidy condition of his study, there is no reason for me to believe that Mr. Tibault's death was anything other than a tragic accident, Dr. Pettigrew." She shrugged nonchalantly. "After all, who would have a motive?"

"Then why are you acting like such a busybody?" he said, losing patience.

She stood to take her leave. "I was just wondering if you could think of any reason why someone would want to kill him."

"I must say you are persistent, Miss Danforth." He smiled ruefully. "I would not like to have you suspect me."

Flattered in spite of herself, Abigail blushed. "I must say, it did occur to me to wonder about Emily."

"Emily?" Pettigrew's brows furrowed.

"She is carrying his child," Abigail said with as much casualness as she could muster. "She might have been angry enough at her predicament to kill him. I know I should be furious if such a terrible thing happened to me."

Pettigrew blushed to the roots of his hair. "Who told you Malcolm Tibault was the father!" he exclaimed. "Did she?"

"I must protect my sources," Abigail replied with a shrug. "Surely you understand?"

"You do not actually believe that Emily—"

"Oh, I pray you, sir, do not mistake my meaning. I suspect no one. I am merely speculating."

"I must ask you to cease and desist in your wild imaginings before you besmirch someone's reputation beyond repair," he exclaimed.

"May I take it that Jeramy Singleton's reputation is above reproach?"

"I cannot personally vouch for everyone Peter Tibault chooses to bring aboard."

"Then it is possible—not probable, mind—merely possible, that he might have a motive for murdering Mr. Tibault that you are not aware of?"

Red faced with fury that she had circled and trapped him so neatly with her logic, he did not answer, but strode toward the door. "I must ask you to leave," he said, reaching for the handle.

Before he could open it, there was a knock on the door. Pettigrew swung it wide.

Standing in the doorway, Emily glanced over her shoulder to make sure no one was about before timidly placing one boot on the threshold. She was about to step into the room when she looked inside and spied Abigail. With a yelp of fright, she whirled around and fled back down the corridor.

12

Despite the laudanum, Maude spent a fretful night. When Abigail opened the curtains at dawn, she pulled the covers over her head to shield herself from the light. Feigning sleep during the onslaught of the maids' appearances, when everyone had left she got out of bed, swept the curtains shut, and resumed her cave under the bedclothes and the modicum of comfort the darkness afforded.

Abigail's criticizing her innocent flirtations with Malcolm Tibault had been exceedingly nettlesome. What did she know about matters of the heart? Had she not openly vowed, ad nauseam, to forswear involvement in the emotions the better to preserve her intellect? How had she known that he would prove himself to be a scoundrel?

Her cheeks burned every time her memory dragged her back to his study. Lured there by the promise of an engraving by Hogarth, truth be told, even when he had promised that Miss Dupree and Mr. Singleton were also expected, she had suspected a ruse. Yet she had been titillated rather than alarmed. Malcolm Tibault had stirred feelings in her that she thought she had buried with her beloved Charles, and she'd been only too happy to dismiss all that she had lectured Abigail against doing, and go to his study alone. When he had closed the door even though the others had not yet arrived, she had merely wondered at his lack of manners in placing her in such a compromising position, and it had not aroused her suspicions. She had continued to trust him to the extent of allowing him to sit next to her on the leather settee.

The rest was a blur. He had lifted her skirts far enough to spy an ankle, of that she was certain, because he had made some lewd comment about her boot lacings. She remembered standing suddenly enough to startle him. But then he had stood, and had actually placed his hand upon her breast.

Maude was no stranger to lovemaking. She and Charles had spent countless hours teasing, laughing, caressing, and languorously delighting each other until their very hearts had entwined. Malcolm Tibault's eyes had held the promise of that same playful tenderness, and Maude had found it irresistible. But when he had suddenly lunged for her it had brought her back to earth with a crash. In all their time together, Charles had never been so crude, nor could she imagine him behaving thus, even in anger. Fortunately, the fan she was carrying was made of sandalwood. She had deliberately chosen it to perfume the air during their tête-à-tête, but when furled it made a formidable weapon. The instant he had touched her, she'd swung it at his face with all her might. He had released her instantly. Not waiting to see the damage she had inflicted, in shock, she had fled.

Just as shocked, he had not followed.

She had spent the afternoon in dread of having to face him again, and wondering if she could get away with hiding in her stateroom until it was time to disembark. Much to her chagrin, her first reaction upon hearing of his death was relief that she'd not have to see him again, and she was almost angry enough to feel that he deserved it, including whatever discomfort he had suffered. But most of all she was disgusted with herself. His eyes had not been filled with the gentleness of a lover of women, but the calculated skill of a seducer. How could she have been so blind? How had Abigail grown so wise?

When she had reached the safety of her stateroom, and realized her earring was missing, she counted herself lucky to have merely lost a piece of jewelry when her heart had been at stake.

* * *

Leaving Pettigrew's surgery, Abigail thought to follow the obviously distraught Emily, and have a word with her before returning to the stateroom to claim Maude. But she soon discovered that when she climbed the stair she thought the girl would have taken, it instead left her stranded on a half-deck, with Emily nowhere in sight. Nor did she find her by going forward and up the next stairway. That move, somehow, had landed her outside the servants' mess hall, with no Emily inside or out. Possessed of an excellent sense of direction, she seldom got lost, yet she was now unsure of the most direct route to her stateroom. Bemused by her predicament, she was about to turn and retrace her steps when she spied a vaguely familiar young man standing at the rail smoking a cigarette. From his cravat to his knickers, he looked the gentleman, and she might have wondered why he was on the servants' deck, except that his cap immediately identified him as a member of the working class. She had seen him but once at the theater, but she recognized him as Malcolm Tibault's Boris.

Few people got to know a man better than his valet, and Abigail had planned to interview him later in the day. Inasmuch as she intended to heed Maude's warning, she had not yet figured out how to create an opportunity without appearing to be a busybody. Suddenly presented with an impeccable excuse for an innocent conversation, she did not hesitate to take advantage of her misadventure, and approached the railing.

Boris tossed his cigarette downwind, doffed his cap, and placed it under his arm. "Lost your way, miss?" he asked respectfully. Extending his free arm, he continued. "The guests' quarters are—"

Ignoring his attempt at being helpful, Abigail continued to walk toward the rail. "As long as I have interrupted your reverie, I wonder if I might have a word with you?"

Boris stiffened. He had much on his mind, and he had just lit the cigarette in the hopes it would still his nerves. Reluctant though he was to comply, his training as a servant was too ingrained to protest the invasion of his privacy, and he joined her at the railing.

Abigail sensed his resistance and wondered at its cause. When she had thought to seek him out, it was to garner information about Tibault. It had not occurred to her that he might be guilty of murder since he had so much to lose by his master's death. Valet to a man of Tibault's wealth and stature was no mean position. The perquisites were many, not the least of which were cast-off clothes of peerless quality and the chance to travel extensively. His position in the household had been an exalted one, and Tibault's death had summarily deposed him. Unless he found employment with Tibault's son, which was unlikely, he was now just another unemployed servant, albeit his résumé would be impressive.

Gazing toward the horizon where sea and sky met in a restless line of blue, she offered her condolences.

"Bad luck voyage," he muttered glumly in response. "We should never have left Colon."

Instantly intrigued, it was all Abigail could do to keep her eyes upon the splendid view. "And why is that?" she asked casually.

It had not been so much the stevedore's drowning that had bothered Boris. The risk of falling overboard was part of a sailor's day, and such an occurrence, while tragic, was not all that uncommon. But the swift manner any questions about the cause of his death had been paid for, and the rush to weigh anchor had given him pause. *The Seascape* was a yacht dedicated to pleasure. No perishable cargo necessitated such a precipitous leave-taking. Suddenly recalling that, as a guest, Abigail knew nothing of the so-called accident, and realizing that he had already said too much for his own good, Boris cast about for a response that would not give away the truth. Without the protection of his master, however unpredictable that might have been, he could not be too careful.

"Something bad was bound to happen." Casting about for a topic that seemed safe enough, he finally hit upon one that was sure to bridge the chasm between servant and guest. "They gave me the heebie jeebies, they did."

"I beg your pardon?" Abigail glanced at him askance.

"Well, I for one, was surprised Mr. Tibault, may God rest his soul, invited them on board. Even if it was only to Cuba."

"Are you referring to the Houdinis?" Abigail asked, wondering what he was driving at.

Boris nodded his head.

Although she had long suspected that servants had opinions about their employer's behavior, she had never before had one confide in her so blatantly. It quite took her breath away. "And the fact that they are show people offended you?" she asked, trying to keep the wonderment at his cheek from her tone.

"Not that, miss—" he hesitated. She had not picked up on his innuendo as swiftly as she should have if she were in agreement with his sentiments. Now he was not so sure he should have begun this conversation either.

"What then?" Abigail persisted.

"You know—" he shrugged meaningfully.

"No, I do not," Abigail exclaimed. "And I have no patience with riddles," she said firmly. "Explain yourself."

"You did not know they were Jews?" he asked with an expression of genuine surprise.

Abigail was appalled. "What?" she exclaimed, scarcely able to believe her ears.

"The Houdinis are Jews—"

"Of course, I knew!" Abigail interrupted. "Ehrich Weiss is scarcely a Christian name."

Boris shrugged as if he had made his point.

"And you thought the voyage was doomed because Mr. Tibault asked Jews to join the cruise." Abigail's voice was flat, her eyes dark.

Boris was completely flummoxed. From her demeanor, it appeared that she was not going to be sympathetic to his anti-Semitism, but neither could he backtrack and tell her what was truly troubling him.

"It offends me when you talk like that," Abigail continued, her tone ominous.

"Beg pardon, miss." Her gaze was fierce, and Boris dared not risk her ire by reminding her that the Jews killed Christ, which he would have done, and hotly, had she been another servant. He sincerely wished the deck would swallow him.

"Mr. and Mrs. Weiss are lovely people, and he is probably the greatest escape artist the world has ever known." Abigail's voice grew deep with anger. "It matters not a whit how they worship." She stepped away from the rail, preparing to take her leave in the direction he had indicated when they'd first met. She had completely lost confidence in his judgment, and had no further use for him. However, she could not resist adding, "You have no right whatsoever to criticize anyone for their religious beliefs." Turning her back on him, she took her leave.

Maude sat at the dressing table to pin her hat in place. The tea had grown cold and, rather than ring for Carlotta, she was intent on going topside for coffee and a muffin and a bit of a lie down upon a chaise on the shady side. But she had no sooner set the final pin in place when Abigail all but burst into the room, her face clouded with disapproval.

Assuming that she was the cause of Abigail's obvious displeasure by having been a slug-a-bed, Maude steeled herself against an assault. "Where have you been?" she asked, with as much disapproval as she could muster since she really had not cared that Abigail had been gone, and, indeed, had welcomed her absence.

Still overwrought by Boris's rude remarks, Abigail ignored Maude's all-too-familiar question. "How dare he!" Strolling over to the canary's cage, her skirts rustled angrily as she whirled around to glare at Maude.

Relieved that it seemed that she was not the cause of Abigail's ill humor, Maude was perfectly willing to let her own question drop. "How dare who do what?" she asked, twisting around in the chair to look at her.

"Mr. Tibault's valet had the nerve to criticize the Houdinis for being Jewish."

"It is not an uncommon sentiment, Miss Danforth." In an effort to soothe Abigail's wrath, Maude kept her own tone mild.

"He is a servant," Abigail exclaimed. "How dare he criticize his betters?"

"His betters?" Maude cocked her head, and her gaze was piercing. "Is he not entitled to feelings?"

Abigail was appalled. "Are you condoning his anti-Semitism?"

"You must learn to keep two issues separate, my dear," Maude said patiently, turning back to face the table to retrieve her gloves. "All I am saying is that everyone has opinions about everything, servant or no." Concentrating on pulling on her gloves, she continued coolly. "If you feel you are better than a valet by virtue of your possession of money, and you believe his opinion misbegotten, perhaps it is your place to teach rather than condemn."

"I do not claim to be better than he," Abigail protested, even more offended than before. "But even you must admit I am better off." Folding her arms across her chest, she added, "Furthermore, I am not a teacher. You cannot expect me to—"

One glove adangle, Maude held up her hands to interrupt. "You do not approve of his opinion?" she asked.

"Certainly not!" Abigail was aghast. "Do you?"

"Certainly not!" Maude exclaimed.

"Well then?"

"But what you said was, how dare he *have* an opinion, not that you disliked it."

Abigail blinked, and grew silent. She had gotten into these entanglements with Maude in the past. Only too aware that she still had much to learn about the ways of the world, but loath to admit that Maude might be right, she sought to change the subject. Sighing heavily, arms still folded, she raked Maude with a reproving glance. "I am pleased that you are finally dressed," she said in a deliberately patronizing fashion. "I spotted Mr. Singleton in the forward salon while finding my way back here. Since I need to speak with him, I would appreciate your accompanying me while I do so."

Interpreting Abigail's sudden switch in topic as a sure sign of victory, if not a complete rout, Maude gathered up her reticule and fan and strolled to the door. Still without a word, she opened it and stood aside for Abigail to precede her.

Having had no breakfast, the rich aroma of coffee as the steward poured it from the silver pot rendered Abigail almost giddy. Another steward used silver tongs to pluck a steaming hot cinnamon bun from its napkin and place it on her side plate. Its sugar glaze melting from the heat and the promise of plump raisins buried in tender, sweet dough destroyed her resolve to refrain from eating while interviewing Mr. Singleton. She began working at her gloves to remove them as she asked, "And how did you know you would find the empress's snuff box in that very spot?"

Maude had removed her gloves the moment that they had joined him at the table set up in the forward salon. She was, therefore, at the ready with her butter knife while listening intently.

"I had traced a copy of Morgan's map," he replied, stirring his coffee. Carefully placing the spoon in the saucer so that it did not clatter, he looked at them soulfully. "I wonder if you ladies can understand what it is like to be sailing away from your dream, instead of making full speed ahead toward it?"

Well acquainted with his frustration, Abigail nodded sympathetically. "Were there others?" she asked.

"A whole chestful," he replied. "It is rumored that one is made from one solid piece of emerald. Another is set in faceted diamonds, none smaller than a carat."

Eyes wide, Maude gasped.

With a slight nod in her direction to acknowledge her appreciation, he continued. "They were being transported from her home in Martinique when the ship went down in a sudden squall."

"And no one has found them in all this time?" Maude said incredulously.

"Their transport was a secret," he replied conspiratorially. "Naturally, after the ship went down, the empress did not want it bandied about that they were on board, or scavengers would have been after them at once."

"How did you discover that they existed?" Abigail asked, after a dainty dab at the corners of her mouth with her napkin.

Jeramy shrugged. "I used to have a partner."

"What happened to him?" she asked, and was much surprised to feel a tug on her sleeve as Maude gave it a yank. She did not, however, betray that she had received such a signal.

"Ahh, he wanted to do things on the cheap." Jeramy shrugged once again. "We had a falling out."

"May I see the snuff box?" Maude asked eagerly.

"That is just it," he replied with a frown. "Mr. Tibault confiscated it. Said it was his because the ship, and everything on it, was his."

"And you handed it over, just like that?" Abigail was astonished. Again, the tug at her sleeve. This time she was sorely tempted to brush Maude's hand away, but refrained because she did not want the treasure hunter to realize anything might be amiss.

"He threatened to have us thrown overboard," Jeramy said, frowning at the memory. "He'd already had a terrific fight with his son that had actually come to blows."

"You did not stop them?" Abigail asked.

Jeramy blushed. "I was not in the room at the time," he replied.

"How do you know—?"

"Believe me, there was a fight," he said roughly. "You would have had to be deaf not to hear it."

"Then who has the snuff box now?"

"Last I saw it, Mr. Tibault put it in the pocket of his dressing gown."

Maude's curiosity got the better of her caution, and she could not resist joining Abigail in her interrogation. "How much would you say it was worth?" she asked eagerly.

"It would keep a man like me, living modestly, for years," he responded. "If I found a modest wife, of course," he finished with a wry smile.

Abigail and Maude exchanged amused glances.

"Ah, but the others!" he exclaimed, leaning close. "Find either one, and my grandchildren would be set for life." Leaning back in his chair, he reached for the spoon, and toyed with it as he spoke. "I must get back before someone else finds out about the spot. Or the currents shift."

"Sounds more difficult than hunting for needles in hay to me." Maude looked at him with a raised brow. "All that sand."

"If the chest is open, indeed it is," he said with a shrug. "But I found one. Why not the others?" Dropping the spoon back into the saucer with a clatter, his voice changed subtly as he said, "But first I must find the one I already found. It is mine, and I mean to have it."

Abigail wondered if he had torn the books out in Malcolm Tibault's study looking for it. But from the look on his face she did not need a yank on her sleeve from Maude to refrain from asking.

The orders from his cohort nearly drove the stowaway mad. He was not, by nature, a killer. The stevedore's death had been a matter of self-preservation. It had all happened so swiftly that it had been done and over with before he realized what he wrought. This time, if he did as he was told, it would be premeditated. He needed to plan. He had to seek this one out, and follow her about. Find her unattended. Preferably near a railing.

That he might be seen throwing her overboard did not concern him. From a distance, he looked like any other swab.

In the off-chance he was spotted in the act, everyone would be too busy manning lifeboats and heaving the ship about to give chase. By the time the search was on, he'd be safe in the hold. And by the time every seaman had been questioned, they'd have docked, and he'd be safe ashore.

But it did bother him that the first had been a man, and this was a lady. Nay—just a young girl. And she was to die only because she had asked too many questions. It wasn't like she really knew anything. Or did she?

13

EVERY TIME PETER closed his eyes, his father's contorted face would appear and scare him awake. Death had made him a very rich man. His thoughts would skitter and slide around this fact. Unable to sleep, he donned dressing gown and slippers, and made his way to his father's—no, *his*—study for some of *his* cognac.

Peter had never seen his father at work, and had no idea how he had occupied his time. Since he seldom had a kind word, Peter had assumed that his father thought him too stupid to learn. He did not know that, secure in the knowledge that his holdings were more than sufficient to support him in his lavish lifestyle, Malcolm Tibault had not cared a candle what happened to his money when he was gone, and had simply seen no reason to train his son in the husbanding of his estates. Consequently, Peter did not know how he was supposed to occupy himself now that he was rich and had no need to waste any more time on an education. Nor had he any idea how to go about making a plan. Until his father had intervened and ruined everything, Ariadne had been his first inspiration to succeed at something, if only to wrest money from his father for her sake. His first taste of ambition had disappeared with her marriage.

Now, suddenly the tables had turned. And, if Ariadne could be believed, he might even win her hand as well. Pouring another two fingers of cognac into the snifter, he wondered if she had really meant it when she'd said she never stopped caring. True, she had risked playing their waltz, but did that mean she still cared? Or had she merely wished to torment him? Had his father really threatened to disinherit him if she would not become his wife? But why had she waited until his death to tell him? Was she worried about her inheritance? When he had been penniless, he had not doubted that she cared. Now he no longer knew what, or who, to believe.

The third snifter of brandy along about first light finally muddled his thoughts so thoroughly there was nothing for it but to curl up on the couch and let the numbness overwhelm him.

The cinnamon bun sat on Jeramy's stomach like so much ballast as he searched *The Seascape* for Peter. Forward, aft, belowdecks, topside—he was nowhere to be found. Before being stopped for coffee by the busybody and her gooseberry, his search had been just as fruitless, and he was beginning to wonder if the young widow might have had him tossed overboard to protect her interest in his father's fortune.

Knowing he'd not find him in Malcolm Tibault's study of all places, but determined to leave no stone unturned, he decided to give it a try. There was no answer to his knock, and he was about to turn away in defeat when he decided to test the door. To his surprise, it opened. More surprising still, upon turning up the wall lamp, he saw Peter sprawled on the leather couch, and for one heart-thumping moment, Jeramy thought he might be dead.

But dead men don't snore, and before he could get close enough to the couch to see that Peter's chest was moving with every breath, or spot the empty brandy snifter, he could hear the evidence of his aliveness even over the creak and groan of the timbers. The room had been restored to order, and only the ink spots that blotched the paneling and stained the carpet, served as a reminder of Malcolm Tibault's violent death. As relieved as he was that he had finally tracked him down, Jeramy was nonetheless angry that it had taken him so long, and he was none too gentle when he shook the sleeping man by the shoulders.

"Wha—?" Elbows out, Peter pulled his hands to his face to ward off the anticipated blow.

"Wake up!" Jeramy all but shouted. "I have been looking for you everywhere. I was beginning to think your stepmother had fair done you in."

Somewhere during his struggle back to consciousness, Peter remembered that his father was dead and, hoping that Jeramy had not noticed his automatic cringe, he swiftly transformed it into a stretch and hand-covered yawn. "Revisiting the scene of the crime?" he asked groggily, pushing himself upright.

Jeramy frowned. "What do you mean by that—?"

"This is where the rich man met his maker." Peter shrugged. He did not ordinarily drink himself to sleep, and his head pounded, his mouth tasted foul, and he was so thirsty he might have been on a desert rather than surrounded by water.

"I had no reason to kill him," Jeramy exclaimed. Striding to the desk, he turned to face the bleary-eyed man. "Look what it got me. We are still sailing away from Martinique." Jabbing his finger at Peter for emphasis, he added, "I want that snuff box. It is mine."

Peter groaned. "You are free to search for it," he said, cradling his aching head in his hands.

Jeramy strode back to the couch and stood over him menacingly. "How do I know you don't have it?"

"For all I know, you have it." Peter glanced up at him. "Come to think of it," he said with a suspicious squint, "all I know about you is that you said you had a piece of map that you said would lead us to a treasure."

"You saw the snuff box with your own eyes," Jeramy said indignantly.

"I saw what you wanted me to see," Peter replied, massaging his head. A drink of water was only a bellpull away, but he did not yet have the strength to stand, nor did he want to ask Jeramy to ring for the steward, as he was fairly certain his next remark would give offense. "Maybe that snuff box was a plant."

"What are you trying to say?" Jeramy stiffened, insulted by the implication.

"What if you had a dirty old snuff box in your possession all along?" Not wanting their discussion to end in fisticuffs, Peter kept his voice reasonable, as if they were discussing the weather. "This whole thing could have been a hoax. Like Houdini. Whoever heard of Empress Josephine's snuff boxes in the first place?"

Struggling to keep his composure, Jeramy strode over to the desk again. "What are you trying to pull?" he asked, turning to face Peter.

"What are *you* trying to pull?"

"I know what you're up to"— Jeramy jabbed his finger at Peter accusingly—"you want that box for yourself."

"What do I want with a stupid snuff box when I have my father's fortune?"

"What about his widow's claim?"

"You heard him," Peter exclaimed. "They were married under the Napoleonic Code. She stands to inherit nothing."

"What were you doing in here?" Jeramy walked back to the couch to stand over him. "Looking for it?"

Peter took an enormous, deep breath and let it out slowly before he said, "This is where my father died."

Instantly contrite, Jeramy sat beside him on the couch. "Sorry," he said, placing his arm around Peter's shoulders. Had anyone else offended him with such accusations, he would have struck him before he'd finished his first sentence. But Peter was now a very wealthy man, and it still might not be too late to persuade him to continue the hunt as an investment. "Don't let us quarrel. I forget how you must feel, losing your father—"

Peter shrugged his arm away. "Make no mistake," he said gruffly. "I am glad he is dead."

"Well, you sure are rich as Croesus."

Peter stood. "He broke my mother's heart," he said, looking

down at Jeramy, his knees trembling. "He ruined the only girl I ever loved." Suddenly turning his face toward heaven, he shook his fists at God and shouted, "I hated the son of a bitch!"

Still seated on the couch, mouth agape, Jeramy could but stare at him.

The motion of the ship did nothing to steady Peter's gait as he staggered to the bellpull. After giving it a good yank, he turned to face Jeramy and said, somewhat sheepishly, "I only wish I had been man enough to tell him to his face before I killed him."

Sails billowed overhead, and padded chaise longues facing the view provided the perfect resting place to while away a few hours in the shade. Maude was already dozing, but Abigail was on the watch for the captain, who, if he kept to his usual schedule, would soon be along on his morning tour. As she waited, she sincerely tried to get into the book she had borrowed, but her thoughts were as restless as the sea, and questions kept surfacing for which she had no answers.

Although she agreed with Maude that Boris had the right to his feelings, she still found it disturbing that he had considered the voyage bad luck because the Weisses had been on board. She could not believe that Malcolm Tibault had shared his valet's prejudice. Not by word or deed had he indicated that he had been anything but amused by the showman. He'd been delighted as a child getting the better of his elders, and had given a credible performance while partaking in the mind-reading trick. Nor had he stinted in his duties as a gentleman with Mrs. Weiss, bestowing upon her more attention than he had given his own wife. Could it be that he had not known his valet's feelings in the matter? Would he have tolerated them if he had? She had never considered Boris as a suspect if indeed Malcolm was murdered, even though he was close enough to his master to have easily administered the poison. The valet had too much to lose, and she found it difficult to believe that his prejudice would be motive enough for murder.

Nor could she ascribe such a crime to Emily, as she, too, stood to lose much by his death if he were the father of her child. She might have been angry enough with him to kill, but who could she turn to for money once he was gone?

The fortune hunter, Jeramy, also seemed a most unlikely villain, unless anger at being so terribly inconvenienced by leaving Martinique had gotten the better of him. But poison was not the usual weapon of choice in a crime of passion. Had Malcolm been killed by a blow to the head, say, or gunshot, she might have placed Jeramy on a list of suspects. Poison, by its very need for some premeditation, seemed to rule him out.

Now Winifred might have used poison. And she probably had an opportunity and method to administer it, but what possible motive could she have?

She did not entirely rule out either the captain or the surgeon since only their motives were obscure. They had both easy access to strychnine and ample opportunity.

Peter was much more likely to be the culprit. He had much to gain, and although he had not seemed all that close to his father, it should not have been too difficult to create an opportunity to give him something to drink or eat that contained the poison.

And then there was the widow. It was here that Abigail faltered. She, herself, had barely escaped a marriage she had not wanted. Who knew what pressures had been put upon the young girl to submit to such an unhappy union. Having grown to like the stalwart wife who had maintained her aplomb without complaint through an extremely trying time, she preferred to believe that Malcolm had eaten some tainted fish, rather than discover that Ariadne had committed murder, no matter the provocation. Nonetheless, she resolved to seek out Emily and question her about her mistress. But first, a word with the captain.

With a quick glance at her watch, and then forward to see if he were nigh, she spotted his ramrod-straight physique just as he turned the corner. Rather than wait until he reached them and perhaps awaken Maude, Abigail set her book aside, threw off the coverlet, and stood.

Seeing her, obviously in wait for him, Thomas Perkins groaned inwardly, and was glad for his full beard and mustache, which, while it sometimes inconveniently hid his smile, also afforded him some modicum of privacy. The voyage had been exceptionally trying to say the least, and the last thing he wished to deal with again was an officious young girl asking a lot of foolish questions. However, he had no choice but to doff his cap as he drew near, and stop.

They exchanged pleasantries, and, hand to hat to keep it safe, Abigail subtly guided him to a spot at the railing. Not knowing how she was going to find out what she really wanted to know, but also curious to see if Boris's prejudice was widespread, she kept her tone noncommittal as she said, "I understand this began as a bad luck voyage."

"And who is your informant?" he asked with raised brow.

"A gentleman's gentleman can know more about his gentleman and his affairs than anyone," Abigail replied, not wishing to name Boris directly nor reveal his prejudice in case the captain did not share it after all. "I remember well as a little girl, if I wanted to know what humor my father was in, I would first ask Kinkade."

Knowing only too well what most impressed servants about their betters, Thomas stroked his beard and sighed. "I suppose Boris could not resist bragging about how Mr. Tibault bought our way out of Colon."

Abigail could scarcely believe her ears. A dozen questions came to mind, but she quelled them all. "He told me no details, of course," she said instead with a coquettish glance that invited him to supply them if he cared to.

"Ah, it was unfortunate." He shook his head sadly. "Put a damper on everyone."

Abigail still could not figure out what he was talking about, and decided to risk a more direct question. "How did it happen?" she asked prettily.

The captain shrugged. "No one knows for sure. He

somehow misstepped and fell overboard. Must have hit his head on the way down. He was gone before we could lower a lifeboat even with the new quick-release gear. Never did find the body. That's what cost Tibault so dear."

"Did you know him?"

"Nah." He looked at her askance. "He was just a stevedore."

"Then you do not think that there could possibly be a connection between his death and Mr. Tibault's?" Abigail asked.

"How could there be?" Thomas drew himself tall, offended by the very idea. "Mr. Tibault was a millionaire many times over. The seaman worked for his monthlies."

"I suppose you are right," Abigail replied thoughtfully. "It is unlikely that a killer would use two different methods for murder."

This was too much for Thomas. Wondering where her father was that he would allow her to be gallivanting about, spouting such queer ideas, he retrieved his hat from under his arm, bowed stiffly, and, excusing himself, clapped it smartly on his head. With that, he turned on his heel and resumed his walk.

Pleased with her newfound information and engrossed in figuring out where it all might fit, Abigail was not the least upset by the suddenness of his departure. It left her free to find Emily without having to explain herself.

Stunned by Peter's confession, Jeramy escaped the study as soon as the steward arrived to take Peter's order for a bromo. Completely at a loss, he roamed topside. Hands clasped behind his back, eyes on the glistening teak deck, oblivious to the beauty that surrounded him, he began to circle the ship on the promenade deck. Blackmail was tempting, but too dangerous to contemplate seriously. Peter might not realize it yet, but his money could buy him anything, including the death of a bothersome blackmailer. Yet surely there must be a way to turn the man's secret into an advantage.

He had gone the length of the ship and turned to port, when it occurred to him that the busybody might be willing to pay for such a secret. She seemed serious enough in her ridiculous quest to become a detective. If the information would help her solve a crime, and establish her reputation, it should be worth money to her. And she must be rich if she was running in Tibault's crowd. She would surely want to pretend that she had figured out Peter's guilt by using clues and not because someone told her the answer, so she'd not be likely to tell on him; therefore, Peter need never know. He did not need much. Just a stake for a boat and crew to get back to Martinique. He was busy trying to figure out how much to ask for when he spotted Abigail and Captain Perkins deep in conversation at the railing. Drawing to a halt, he sidestepped into the shadows cast by the deckhouse, the better to observe them without being seen.

They seemed so engrossed that the conversation would not be finished any time soon. He dared not interrupt, since privacy was essential if his plot was to succeed, even to the point of not being seen approaching her, and he decided to turn back toward starboard. Time enough to see the young detective later. Meanwhile, had not Peter given him permission to search for the cabochon snuff box? If Ariadne was not about, and Tibault's rooms were unlocked, he would search them. It was unlikely that it would still be in the dead man's dressing gown pocket, but it was worth a try.

The ubiquitous white-clad sailors might have been fish in the sea for all Jeramy noticed their presence. Much like the attendants on stage in Houdini's disappearing act, it would never have occurred to him to count how many were on duty on any given watch. They all looked alike, and since they were on board to work, guests on the yacht tended not to notice their presence at all.

But one white-clad fellow was very different from the others. The stowaway was also watching Abigail, and had she been standing so near the railing unattended rather than with the captain and no witnesses about, he would have thrown her overboard. He'd have no need to strike a blow. Even if she could swim, which was doubtful, even if the lifeboat were lowered swiftly, and even if the ship were to heave to smartly, her high-laced boots and heavy skirts would surely drag her down before she could be rescued.

Abigail had long before discovered that sometimes the long way around could prove to be shortest, and rather than seek out Emily herself, she returned to her stateroom to ring for Jacqueline. Upon receiving no answer, she rang the servants' parlor. In due course, Carlotta appeared, since any bell rung in the parlor by a female guest was hers to answer. She allowed as how Emily was not in the parlor.

Jacqueline was catching up on some sewing in the parlor, but not knowing whether it was Maude or her mistress who rang, she had remained there. She and Carlotta had agreed that if it proved to be Abigail, and it was she that Abigail was ringing for, then Abigail need only ring once more, and Jacqueline would appear in a trice.

When in due course Jacqueline appeared, she confirmed that Emily had not been in the parlor, and readily agreed to lead Abigail to their quarters.

Following Jacqueline through the half-deck twists and turns to reach her cabin, Abigail was much impressed that her maid had learned her way about so quickly. Intent upon memorizing her way back in case she needed to return alone, she was completely unprepared for the awful sight that greeted them when Jacqueline opened the door. Although the oil lamp flickered on dim, Emily's contorted body lay in plain view, sprawled on the floor, much as Malcolm Tibault's had been.

Jacqueline drew breath to scream, but before she could utter a sound, Abigail clapped a hand over her mouth, shoved her into the room, and, through a tangle of skirts, kicked the door shut.

▽

14

WITH HER HAND still clasped to Jacqueline's mouth, Abigail bent as close to her maid's ear as the large brim of her hat would allow. Appreciating that Jacqueline might have need of some release from the shock, she whispered, not unkindly, "Grab a pillow and scream into that, if scream you must."

The sympathy in Abigail's tone quelled Jacqueline's impulse to yank her mistress's hand away, which she could have easily done physically even though Abigail was taller than she. Although her eyes remained wide from the shock of their gruesome discovery, she nodded her head to indicate that she would not scream.

Satisfied that Jacqueline would not make any undue hue and cry, Abigail took her hand away and, lifting her skirts, tiptoed the few steps to reach Emily's body.

Her back was arched and her hands were balled into fists as they clutched at the beltline of her apron. Her head was thrown back, and with her mouth pulled up wide in a grimace that might easily be mistaken for a drunken smile, and cap askew at a rakish angle, she looked as if she might have been having a rowdy time of it instead of dying in excruciating pain.

Jacqueline remained by the door. Her voice was unnaturally high as she spoke. "Shall I go and—"

"Shhhh!" Abigail frowned. Yanking at her gloves, she stooped over the body for a closer look. Controlling her own desire to retch from the sight and smell of vomit that had begun to dry on Emily's chin and apron front, she placed her hand upon Emily's throat to feel for a pulse.

Horrified that her mistress was actually touching the corpse, and puzzled by her insistence upon silence, Jacqueline nonetheless obeyed and drew closer to her, the better to be heard. Her gaze fixed straight ahead so that she would not witness the horrible sight, she whispered, "Shall I fetch the captain, miss?"

Busy examining Emily's body, Abigail did not look up, but shook her head vehemently. "She has not been dead for very long," she replied. "Her body is still warm."

"No, miss?" Jacqueline could scarcely believe her ears. When they had come upon Mr. Tibault's body, she had been halfway to the bridge to fetch the captain by now.

"He is the last person I would have find out." The severe convulsions had caused a premature rigor mortis to set in, and Abigail was having difficulty examining Emily's hands for signs of a struggle.

Although trained to obey without question, this situation was so extraordinary that Jacqueline quite forgot herself. "But why, miss—?"

"He will no doubt insist upon tossing her body overboard," Abigail interrupted crossly, too preoccupied to properly scold her maid for pestering her with questions.

Jacqueline was aghast, and it was all she could do to keep her voice at a whisper. "But that is the law."

"It is not law," Abigail replied. Satisfied that there were no other signs of violence on Emily's body, she stood and drew on her gloves. "Bodies are disposed of because of the swift putrification of flesh in the tropics." Brushing at her skirts, she added, "But we are due in port soon, and I would like the officials there to examine her body for poison. It is so unlikely as to be improbable that she, too, ate tainted food."

"But we are not due to land until morning, miss."

"That is less than twenty-four hours from now. She will keep for that long." Abigail gestured toward the bunks. "Quick," she said. "Fetch the sheet off the bed."

Suspecting Abigail's intention, Jacqueline was too horrified to move. "The sheet, miss?"

"Yes," Abigail said with mounting impatience. "We will wrap her body in it."

"*Sacrebleu!*" Jacqueline exclaimed, clapping her hands to her cheeks, eyes wide with horror.

"Do not be so squeamish." Abigail frowned as she waved her hand in the direction of the bunk beds. "She won't bite."

"Oh, but miss, I cannot," Jacqueline wailed, her voice rising.

"Shhhh!" Fingertips to lips in warning, Abigail frowned. "Do not be a goose. She cannot hurt you."

Jacqueline moved toward the bunk bed so reluctantly, she might have been going to her own funeral.

"Move!" Abigail said impatiently. "I have much to do when we leave here."

Wishing she could protest Abigail's outrageous demands, Jacqueline took out her frustration on the bed sheet as she yanked it from its moorings. Scooping it up so that it did not trail on the floor, she turned and faced Abigail.

"Come," Abigail beckoned impatiently. "Together we can lift Emily onto the bottom bunk."

Jacqueline hugged the sheet close, unable to move. "But where shall I sleep?" she asked, her voice aquiver with fear that she knew the answer.

"On the top bunk." Hand outstretched to take the sheet, Abigail moved toward her frozen maid.

"Oh, miss, I could not." The color drained from Jacqueline's face as she relinquished the sheet.

"Oh very well," Abigail replied with a heavy sigh. "You can curl on the chaise with Miss Cunningham and me if it comes to that." With no experience whatever in making beds, Abigail's attempts to drape the sheet over the body were so inept that Jacqueline was compelled to take over the task. Together they rolled the body over so that it was enshrouded. It proved heavier and more awkward to maneuver than Abigail had anticipated, but with much grunting and no little tripping over their long skirts, they managed to drag it across the room and, heaving it onto the bottom bunk, shove it deep into the shadows.

Following Abigail's instructions, Jacqueline arranged the covers around her body so that she would appear to be asleep should anyone crack open the door and peek in. Of course, the jig would be up should they approach the bed.

Even as they were dragging the body across the room, Abigail spied the china cup and saucer on the night table. While Jacqueline was thus occupied with the bedclothes, she stooped over to examine it more closely. Dregs of chocolate milk remained in the bottom. Opening the drawer to the night stand, she made room for it beside the Bible.

"Excuse me, miss," Jacqueline said softly as Abigail closed the drawer. "What will you tell Mrs. Tibault?"

Abigail paused thoughtfully for a moment. "Nothing."

"Not even tell her that Emily is asleep in her bed?"

"Especially that," Abigail exclaimed. "What if she came to take a look, pray? If asked, and only if asked, you must pretend that you know nothing of Emily's whereabouts."

Jacqueline hesitated. It was a virtual certainty that once Mrs. Tibault knew that Emily was dead, she would insist on an answer to her invitation to join her staff, and she needed advice desperately. "May I tell you the secret, and you will not be angry?"

"Yes, of course." Offended by Jacqueline's implication that she was temperamental, Abigail did not realize that her impatient frown seemed to belie her words. "What is it?"

Not at all sure that Abigail would not become angry enough to give her the boot, Jacqueline hesitated again.

"Out with it," Abigail exclaimed. "I have much to see to."

"Mrs. Tibault . . . ah . . . well . . . ah . . . she asks me if I will be her maid."

Had she not so much on her mind, Abigail might have made much of her hostess's perfidy. As it was, she wanted to know only one thing. "You told her no, of course?" It sounded more like statement of fact than question.

"Ah, no, miss." Jacqueline blushed furiously.

Abigail was stunned. "You told her yes?" She could scarcely get the words out.

"No, miss," Jacqueline said, realizing her mistake. "I do not tell her anything."

"But you mean to tell her no, do you not?" Abigail asked, surprised at how much her maid's answer meant.

"Oh, yes, miss . . . I just do not know how—"

"How long ago was this?" Abigail asked, suddenly curious.

"The first night I take Emily's place."

"That long ago?" Abigail frowned. "You should have come to me at once." She was about to ask her maid why she had not, when she realized there were more urgent matters at hand. "If Mrs. Tibault asks you to tend her for dinner, you must tell her of your decision. Furthermore, you must be a good actress and not let on about Emily's demise."

"Yes, miss," Jacqueline replied, hoping she'd be equal to the task. "But what do I do now, miss?"

"Return to the parlor and get on with your sewing." With a final glance about the room, Abigail started for the door. "I would recommend that you eat nothing until we reach port," she said, suddenly turning to face her maid.

Eager to quit the room, Jacqueline very nearly bumped into her mistress, but stopped just in time. "Nothing, miss?" she asked piteously. "I am fairly starved."

"Very well, then," Abigail said impatiently. "Some fruit perhaps. No pineapple, because you do not know who prepared it. A banana or an orange should be safe enough, but see to it that you peel them yourself. And scrub your apple well."

"What about the tea, miss?"

"Absolutely not," Abigail exclaimed. "And taste the water before you swallow. If it seems bitter, spit it out no matter the breach in etiquette. There may be a killer loose on board this ship. Who knows where he—or she—will strike again."

"You what!" Maude sat bolt upright on the chaise. Immediately wide awake, she stared at Abigail in shocked disbelief.

"Shhhh!" Seating herself on the edge of the chaise facing Maude, Abigail held gloved fingertips to her lips. Glancing around to see if their conversation had been overheard, she whispered, "But Captain Perkins or Dr. Pettigrew would have her body tossed overboard if I told them."

"You cannot hide a body like that," Maude cried. "What . . . what if it begins to smell?"

"I am preserving evidence," Abigail replied firmly. "Besides, we will be landing in New Orleans before another day passes."

"Can you not feel how warm it is getting?"

"Exactly so," Abigail exclaimed excitedly. "It is much too humid for a cup of hot chocolate."

"What does hot chocolate—?"

"I found a teacup on the night stand with chocolate coating the bottom. For one thing it was a good china cup. Not one that Emily would normally have access to. She'd be in a goodly amount of trouble were she caught using one."

"Why could that not just as easily mean that she was bent on committing suicide, pray?"

"What makes you say that?" Abigail frowned.

Maude shrugged. "She would be heedless of the consequences."

Abigail shook her head in disagreement. "More likely it means that someone came to her quarters and served her."

"Then why would they not remove the incriminating evidence?"

Abigail hesitated but a moment before responding, "If he—or she—was interrupted. Or they might leave it behind knowing that others would assume, as you did, that she committed suicide. Chocolate would disguise the taste of strychnine."

"It is much more likely that she committed suicide, Miss Danforth," Maude said. "After all, she was in a dreadful pickle." She shrugged. "Besides, who would want her dead?"

"Peter Tibault might—if he is the father of her child," Abigail said. "She would be an enormous embarrassment to him, now that he is a wealthy man."

"But then he could simply buy her off, could he not?"

"If not Mr. Tibault, then his widow."

"But why?"

"I do not pretend to have all the answers, Miss Cunningham." Abigail stood and looked down at Maude. "But two people have died under very similar circumstances, and I do not believe that either one ate tainted food or committed suicide."

"You are truly convinced that both of them were poisoned, are you not?" Maude returned her level gaze.

Abigail nodded without speaking.

"Well then," Maude said, patting the spot by her side for Abigail to sit again. "Is there anything I can do to help?"

"I need to interview Mr. Tibault," Abigail said, shaking her head to refuse Maude's invitation to sit on the chaise. "I wonder if I might persuade you to accompany me?"

"If you will first excuse me for one moment," Maude said, tossing the coverlet aside to gain her feet. "I have been sitting here so long I must run a personal errand." Gathering her fan and reticule, she continued. "If you do not mind waiting for me for a moment, I will rejoin you as soon as I am done."

Standing at the railing awaiting Maude's return, Abigail's gaze might have been on the panorama of land hoving into view on the horizon, but her mind was on her thoughts. Sailors climbing about on the rigging, running hither and yon on mysterious errands, were so much a part of the life of the ship that she paid scant attention to the white-clad man who approached her. It was unusual for one to use the guests' promenade to get from one place to another, but he carried a bucket, and she would have assumed, if she had thought of it at all, that he was on his way to perform some task, and would take no more notice of her presence than she did of his.

But the stowaway had no intention of passing her by. Having already made sure he would not be observed, he slowed his brisk pace as he drew near and stopped altogether when he reached her. Turning to face her, he dropped the bucket, stooped, and, arms wide, lunged.

Hearing the bucket strike the deck, Abigail spun around. But too late.

Crouched low, he grabbed her around the thighs, and scooped her up off her feet. She was a mite heavier than he had anticipated, and he hesitated for an instant to better balance himself to heave her overboard.

Suddenly finding herself high in the air with nothing between her back and the roiling sea below, held by a part of her anatomy that had never before been touched by a man, Abigail screamed. Outraged by the indignity, in a purely reflex motion, she flung her arms wide. Tethered to her wrists, her fan and reticule flew through the air as she brought her hands back together with all her might, slamming them against his ears.

Pain exploded like a lightning bolt in his head. Screaming in agony, the stowaway dropped her to grab his head.

Although Abigail had boxed his ears as hard as she could to gain her freedom, she was unprepared for how quickly he let her go, and was off-balance when her feet struck the deck. She fell to her knees, which were somewhat cushioned from harm by her skirts. Even through her gloves, her hands stung—not from stopping her fall on the deck so much as from their contact with his ears. Knowing she could not gain her feet and flee before he recovered sufficiently to give chase, she shoved herself up so that she was kneeling and, seeking to bring him down with her, threw her arms around, and shoulder into, his shins.

Hoping that fresh air would help cure his hangover, Peter had begun his stroll on the port side. He had no sooner reached starboard when he had glanced ahead and seen the sailor approaching Abigail, who was taking her leisure at the railing. Nothing unusual in that, and he had started to turn his attention toward landfall when the sailor suddenly stopped in his tracks and attacked her. Startled out of his doldrums, hand upon hat to steady it, cane slashing the air in front of him, he had dashed forward crying, "Unhand her!"

Thrown completely off balance by Abigail's tackle, the stowaway crashed to the deck.

The moment he started to fall, Abigail released her hold on his shins, and began to scramble to her feet.

The pain in his head had subsided, but the stowaway was so astonished to find himself flat on his back that he was unaware that Peter was racing to the rescue. With Abigail still so near, he thought he need only get up, grab her, and try again. Thus he had rolled over, face down, to push himself upright with his hands when the first blow to his shoulders fell.

"Take that!" Peter shouted as he brought his walking stick down on the stowaway's shoulders. "And that!" he exclaimed, striking him again and again.

The stowaway tried to put his arms up to protect himself to no avail.

"Stop!" Abigail shouted. Upon seeing Peter's approach, she had scurried out of range of his cane, and gotten to her feet. But seeing the crazed look in his eye, she dared not draw too close to him to try and still his arm.

All the pent-up rage that he had ever felt when his father had beaten him came rushing up as Peter swung the cane high and struck repeatedly. He cared nothing for where his blows fell, or that after one had landed solidly on the back of the man's head, he had fallen quite still.

It was not until Jeramy had come running up and grabbed his arm that he stopped.

Grateful that Peter had come to her rescue but sickened by his violence, Abigail signaled to one of the sailors who had also drawn near, attracted by the commotion. "Fetch Dr. Pettigrew!" she cried.

Realizing that he might have killed the man, Peter dropped

his cane on the deck and, putting his hands to his face, began to sob.

Eager to find out who had put him up to throwing her overboard, and unwilling to wait for the doctor to arrive to pronounce him fit to talk, Abigail knelt by the white-clad figure to examine him.

"Allow me, Miss Danforth." Jeramy grabbed her unceremoniously by the elbow, and hauled her to her feet. Before she could protest, he was bending over the prostrate figure and, handkerchief at the ready to stanch the bleeding from the wound on the back of the man's head, turned him over to take a pulse. "Oh, my God!" he exclaimed upon seeing the man's face. "It is Philip!"

▽

15

"WHO IS PHILIP?" Abigail asked, her curiosity winning out over feelings as roiled as the sea. "How do you know him?" Realizing she must look a fright after being so roughly handled, she automatically straightened her hat by feel, and neatened her skirts as she looked down at Jeramy, awaiting his answer.

Still kneeling over the body, Jeramy twisted himself around to look up at her. "He was my partner for almost four years, Miss Danforth."

Peter took his hands away from his face and, bringing his horrified sobs under control, looked down at Jeramy. "Your partner!" he exclaimed, his voice cracking. "You never told me you had a partner."

"We split up," Jeramy said as he adjusted himself to tenderly cradle Philip's head in his lap. "Philip was the one who found the map."

Several sailors hovered close by. One, bolder than his companions, stood close enough to overhear what was happening, and passed the word.

"I had no idea he was on board." Jeramy looked up at the circle of faces that leaned over him and Philip. "I swear it."

"How did he get on board?" Abigail asked. "Where has he been hiding?"

"You should ask Mr. Tibault those questions, Miss Danforth." Jeramy placed his free hand on his heart. "I swear, until this moment I thought Philip was in Panama."

"Why ask me?" Peter said, backing away a step or two. "I never laid eyes upon that man before this minute."

"You are lying!" Jeramy cried, immediately suspicious that Peter had planned to two-time him all along. "Philip had to know someone on board who would hide him."

"Not I!" Peter protested. "Ask him," he said, pointing to the wounded man.

Before Jeramy could protest again, the circle parted to allow Amos Pettigrew through.

The doctor knelt next to Jeramy, and all speculations ceased as everyone watched him check for vital signs. After a second try for a pulse at the wounded man's throat, Amos placed a sympathetic hand on Jeramy's shoulder and shook his head sadly.

"Are you sure?" Jeramy asked.

Amos shook his head again and, gaining his feet, announced to anyone who cared to listen, "The man is dead."

Again, the news was spread.

Carefully placing Philip's head, with his blood-soaked handkerchief underneath, on the deck, Jeramy got to his feet. The thighs of his trousers where Philip's head had been were soaked through with blood. "You killed him!" he cried, starting for Peter.

But Amos stood between them. While the doctor was not a large man, he had a commanding demeanor, and he did not hesitate to place a restraining hand on the thin man's chest to block his progress.

Seeing that the doctor was going to protect him, Peter stood his ground. "I do not care if he was your partner, he tried to throw Miss Danforth overboard," he cried, looking about him for support.

"Philip would never hurt a fly!" Jeramy shouted, shaking his fist. "You put him up to it!"

"Never!" Peter exclaimed. "Why would I do such a thing!"

"To have an excuse to kill him." Jeramy shot a swift glance at Abigail. Busy searching for the snuff box, he'd had no chance to tell her about Peter's confession, and it pained him mightily to forfeit his chance for recompense. But it was clear to him that Peter was going to get away with killing his partner because he did it to save a damsel in distress, and he could not bear to see the man go free. "You killed your father!" he cried. "Philip knew and was trying to blackmail you."

Amos kept his restraining hand on the fortune hunter's chest as he looked at Peter. "Is that true?"

"Of course not!" Peter exclaimed.

"But you confessed!" Jeramy cried, pointing a finger in the general direction of the book-lined study. "I heard you myself."

"I only meant that I wished I had killed him," Peter cried, his hands spread wide to protest his innocence. "I struck down your friend to save Miss Danforth from certain death. Doesn't that count for anything?"

"He had released me," Abigail said coolly, doubting that Peter would have used poison to dispatch his father when he had such a violent temper at the ready. Although tempted, she refrained from mentioning Emily's demise until she could have a quiet moment to question him alone. But it did occur to her to wonder if she were doubting his guilt just because it had been Jeramy who had exposed him, and not due to any cleverness on her part. "There was no reason for you to continue beating him." With a sideways glance at Jeramy, she added, "Unless, of course, you had some reason to prevent him from talking as Mr. Singleton seems to think."

"You must believe I did not mean to," Peter said. "I was striking him about the shoulders—his head got in the way." Looking about for a friendly face, he spotted Maude, who had just insinuated herself into the circle beside Abigail, near the railing. "I did not want him to get up and attack Miss Danforth again."

"It is true, Dr. Pettigrew," Abigail said, as much to inform Maude as to confirm Peter's story. "The man did try to throw me over the side."

Maude gasped.

Not wishing to have Maude rub it in about being right,

or stop to fill her in on all that had transpired during her brief absence, Abigail silenced her companion by grabbing her hand and, concealing it from view of the others in the folds of her skirts, squeezed it. "If you had not stopped him, Mr. Tibault, he might have succeeded," she continued. This was neither the time nor the place to hurl accusations at anyone. Better she wait until they were all ashore with proper officials about for protection. "You saved my life," she said graciously. "And for that I shall be eternally grateful."

"I am most heartily sorry I killed your partner, Mr. Singleton," Peter said, with a slight bow. "Despite what you think of me, I would have preferred to find out who put him up to his attack upon Miss Danforth." Straightening his cravat, he said, "And I swear to you that I did not kill my father."

Before Jeramy could respond, the captain appeared, his face a stern mask of disapproval. "What's this I hear?" he asked, looking to Amos for an answer. "I can see by her presence that Miss Danforth was not thrown overboard." Looking down at her feet where the dead man lay, he said, "Oh, I say, Dr. Pettigrew, is he—?"

"Quite," Amos interrupted.

Releasing Maude's hand, Abigail stepped forward. "Mr. Tibault was rather more enthusiastic with his cane than he need have been when coming to my rescue," she replied before Amos could respond. "I suppose you will want to toss his body overboard at once?"

"Not at all, Miss Danforth," the captain replied with a sweep of his hand to indicate landfall in the distance. "That faint line over there is the Gulf coast hoving into view. The body will keep until we land."

"If it is all the same to you, sir," Jeramy said. "Philip would have preferred to be buried at sea."

The captain shrugged his approval and, signaling to one of the officers who had accompanied him, turned to give him orders.

"But first, I insist you arrest that man," Jeramy said, pointing at Peter.

Captain Perkins stiffened. He was not about to risk his tentative hold on his position by performing so rash an act. "But does not everyone agree that the man he killed tried to kill Miss Danforth?"

"Not for that," Jeramy exclaimed, shaking an accusing finger at Peter. "He told me, flat out, that he killed his father."

Peter hung his head, his voice suddenly so low Abigail could scarcely hear him above the wind as he said, "I only wished I had."

"We will be landing soon," the captain replied. Impressed that Abigail had been right after all, he was nonetheless unwilling to jeopardize his standing with the family by being the one to seize Peter, even if he were guilty of patricide. "Time enough for arrests dockside, if necessary."

Throwing up his hands in disgust, Jeramy excused himself to change his blood-soaked trousers before the ceremony for Philip.

A much relieved Abigail duly noted, by inference, that . Emily's body should make the rest of the trip undetected. There could be no doubt that Peter killed the man called Philip with his cane since she had witnessed the deed, but discovering why he did it did not depend upon finding anything on Philip's body, and she was content that he be buried at sea. Peter might even have killed Emily if he was the father of her child. And although he protested his innocence, he certainly might have killed his father. But why poison? With a high sign to Maude, who stood at the railing, to join her in the salon to wait for the plank and shroud to arrive and Mrs. Tibault to be informed, she started for the doorway. Except for her suspicions that Malcolm and Emily had both died of strychnine poisoning, she could think of no connection between any of the deaths. It was highly unlikely that Jeramy's ex-partner had been hidden without someone in an important position aboard the ship being aware of his presence—perhaps even Malcolm Tibault himself. It was also unlikely that he was acting on his own when he tried to kill her. She needed no warning from Maude to keep her peace—she had seen with her own eyes the violence that Peter Tibault was capable of.

A shaken Peter followed the ladies into the salon and ordered a waiting steward to bring whiskey. Once the ladies were seated, he all but fell into a chair beside Maude.

While the captain remained outside to see to it that the body was prepared for burial, Amos picked up Peter's walking stick and, wiping the bloodstains off the silver head with his handkerchief, joined the others in the salon. He held out the cane for Peter to claim. "You dropped this, Mr. Tibault?" he said, hoping to lighten the gloom.

With a growl deep in his throat, Peter snatched the cane from his hand. Bolting from his chair, he dashed outside holding the cane high much like a javelin thrower in a contest, and threw it overboard with all his might. As it arced through the air he collapsed, sobbing, onto the railing.

Before Peter had reached the doorway, Amos realized how tactless he had been. Excusing himself to the ladies, he hurried after Peter and stood quietly beside him for a moment to allow the distraught man to compose himself before placing a comforting arm about his shoulders.

Annoyed by Peter's disappearance, yet eager to take advantage of their unexpected moment of privacy, Abigail turned to Maude to test her theories regarding the possibility of his being guilty of not one, but three, possibly four, murders. But before she could speak they were interrupted by a high-pitched wail issuing from the guests' companionway. Both ladies turned their attention toward the sound, and were surprised to see Jacqueline emerge. Abigail wondered what new disaster had befallen the accursed ship to justify her maid's unprecedented use of the wrong stairs.

Cap askew, skirts held ankle high the better to run, Jacqueline did not see them seated in the shadows as she dashed for the doorway that led to the deck outside, wailing as if the devil himself gave chase.

"Jacqueline Bordeaux!" Concerned that people might think she allowed her servants to behave in such an unseemly manner unchecked, Abigail stood, the better to be seen.

Upon hearing her name, Jacqueline almost fell in her effort to stop, and turned to peer in the direction of the source.

"What has come over you!" Abigail exclaimed in her most imperious tones.

"*Mon Dieu!*" Jacqueline cried, staring into the shadows. "Is that you, Miss Danforth?"

"Of course, it is I," Abigail replied indignantly.

"Oh, Miss Danforth!" Jacqueline cried, hurrying closer. "I am so happy to see you. They say you are the man overboard."

"Who told you that?" Abigail whispered with fingertips to her lips to get Jacqueline to lower her voice.

"The steward, miss," Jacqueline whispered. "He comes to Mrs. Tibault's—"

"You were supposed to remain in the servants' parlor," Abigail interrupted impatiently. "What were you doing in Mrs. Tibault's quarters?"

"She calls me to ready her for tea, miss—"

"Did she ask about Emily?"

"No, miss, nary a word."

"Curiouser and curiouser." Abigail frowned. "Where is Mrs. Tibault now?"

Jacqueline lowered her gaze to stare at her toes.

"Speak up," Abigail whispered harshly. "This is no time to beat about bushes."

"Beg pardon, miss, I thought you were dead. I leave her with her hair down."

After a quick glance outside to reassure herself that neither Peter nor Amos had noticed Jacqueline's arrival, and that the captain was too far forward of the salon to have seen her, Abigail signaled to Maude to remain seated. Taking Jacqueline by the arm, she steered her toward the servants' stairs. "Go below at once," she said rapidly. "Borrow a cap and apron with *The Seascape*'s ribbons. Send Carlotta to the salon so that she is here before you return. When you come back, stay hidden but within earshot."

"Hide, miss?"

"Dressed in the Tibaults' livery, you will look enough like Emily if you stay in the shadows. I want to see Mr. Tibault's reaction when he thinks she might still be alive," Abigail replied.

"But Mrs. Tibault, miss?"

"I daresay she will arrive shortly without your ministrations," Abigail said. "Now hurry."

As she hurried back to Maude for a few words, it occurred to Abigail to wonder what Ariadne's reaction would be if she found Maude alone. Eager to test her theory, she stooped behind Maude's chair, all the while explaining that she wanted to see what Ariadne would say upon believing her to be dead. She had ducked her head to conceal her hat not a moment too soon, since a black-clad Ariadne emerged from the same companionway that Jacqueline had used by mistake. Pausing at the top, holding on to her hat, which was not as secure as it should have been, she searched the salon and, spotting Maude, hurried straightaway to her side. "Oh, I am so very sorry to hear about Miss Danforth," she cried. "What a terrible tragedy."

Maude held a handkerchief to her face without speaking, stalling for time.

"I heard that she fell overboard." Looking outside, the young widow spotted Peter and the doctor at the railing. "Have the lifeboats been lowered? Why have we not turned about?" She turned as if to leave.

Abigail swiftly gained her feet. "Who told you I was dead?" she asked.

"Miss Danforth!" Ariadne exclaimed, returning her hand to her unsteady hat. "Oh, I say, what a relief!" She paused for an instant. "What were you doing, hiding back there?" she asked suspiciously. "You gave me such a fright."

Abigail held her reticule aloft by way of explanation, but before she could speak Ariadne had turned away and was dashing toward the doorway with such speed that her veil came untied.

Abigail and Maude followed outside to find the now familiar tableau of a plank set on the railing with a shrouded body on it, held firm by sailors who waited, solemn-faced, for the captain to commit it to the deep.

"Let me see," Ariadne cried, rushing to the captain's side.

Since she had not asked for a last look at her husband, the captain was surprised that she wanted to view a stranger. "It is not a pretty sight, Mrs. Tibault," he said while nodding at a sailor to cut open the shroud.

"This is my ship now," she replied as the sailor did as he was told. "I must be apprised of everything . . . " Her voice trailed off as she gazed at the dead man's face.

Abigail hurried to gain a vantage point to watch the widow's expression when she looked upon the dead man, but the heavy veiling had all fallen in front of her face and shielded it from view.

"Do you know him, Mrs. Tibault?" the captain asked as Amos and Peter drew close.

"I never saw him before." She turned to Peter. "Who is he?"

"Mr. Singleton's partner," Peter replied. "Apparently they had broken up."

"Where is Mr. Singleton?" Ariadne asked, looking about. "Did he know his partner was on board?"

Before Peter could answer, Jeramy appeared, freshly attired, with Boris in tow.

With land drawing ever closer, and little time to spare, the captain called for silence. Intoning a few words over the body, he signaled to the sailors to tilt the plank.

Ariadne folded her hands in prayer. Scarcely had the body struck the water when the wind caught her unattended hat and swirled it overboard.

Dismissing his men, the captain offered Ariadne his arm to escort her to the salon as if nothing were amiss even though the few pins in her hair soon lost their grip in the wind, and her long blond hair trailed down her back in a manner more fitting to the privacy of a bedchamber.

Boris and Carlotta made themselves scarce as the others followed the captain and Ariadne into the salon, whereupon the captain excused himself to return to the bridge to see *The Seascape* safely into port.

Ariadne declined to be seated even as she insisted the gentlemen do so. They of course refused, but Maude settled herself comfortably at once.

Suddenly wondering if Ariadne and Peter were in cahoots, and desperate to test her theory before Ariadne disappeared down the companionway to tend her hair never to reappear, Abigail called out, loud enough for all to hear, "Would you actually have me killed just so you could have my maid?"

"Miss Danforth!" Peter cried. "What a terrible thing to say!"

Duly noting that he came to Ariadne's defense quickly enough, Abigail watched Ariadne's expression, which was now clearly visible without the widow's veil. She seemed composed, but before she could respond, Abigail addressed Peter. "Why doesn't she use Emily instead of my maid, pray?" she asked, pointing an accusatory finger at Ariadne.

"Emily has been indisposed for most of this trip, Miss Danforth," Ariadne replied reasonably enough.

"She is not indisposed now." Praying that Jacqueline had obeyed her instructions, she continued confidently. "There she is!"

It was all Abigail could do to keep herself from applauding when Jacqueline stepped inside the doorway on the starboard side. With the sun behind her and the distinctive stripes on her cap and apron, she might have passed for Emily.

"But that is impossible!" Ariadne cried, her composure completely destroyed.

"Impossible?" Abigail asked, drawing close to the distraught widow. "Why, impossible, pray?"

As the realization of what she'd said struck her, Ariadne

glared at Abigail. Knowing she'd already said too much, Ariadne all but shouted the words."Emily is dead!"

The gentlemen, Peter included, Abigail duly noted, stared at Ariadne in shocked silence.

"No one knew that but the killer, Mrs. Tibault," Abigail said gently, certain now that she had the guilty party.

"She might have committed suicide!" Ariadne cried, looking about wildly. "Everyone knows she was carrying my husband's baby."

"That was no reason to kill her," Amos said. Convinced that Ariadne had done it, he suddenly decided to end his long silence before any more damage was done. "I was going to insist upon an abortion."

"She would never agree," Ariadne interrupted.

"She would have when I told her that Mr. Tibault had syphilis," Amos replied.

All color drained from Ariadne's face, and she staggered. "My husband had syphilis?" She could scarcely get the words out.

Dashing forward, Amos caught her before she fell and, holding her close, helped her to the settee. While Abigail took the seat next to her, he sat in the closest chair and chaffed her wrist.

Maude rummaged in her reticule for smelling salts, but when she found none she stayed put. Ariadne seemed to be reviving, and she did not want to miss a word.

Utterly fascinated, both Jeramy and Peter pulled chairs close and also sat.

Ariadne mopped at her eyes with a handkerchief, and with her hair pouring over her shoulders and down her back, she looked more like an adorable child than a killer. "I am doomed," she sobbed.

"Did you kill your husband because he was going to divorce you?" Abigail asked, chastising herself for having allowed her sympathies toward the young girl to cloud her judgment, and determined not to be taken in any longer by Ariadne's doll-like appearance.

Ariadne shook her head as she struggled for composure.

"Why, then?" Abigail persisted, certain now that Ariadne's response meant the motive was wrong, not the deed.

"He gave me no choice." Ariadne shrugged, and let out a heavy sigh. With the specter of her own death looming large, there was no longer any reason to lie. "He insisted we leave Martinique."

Jeramy sat on the edge of his chair. "You and Philip were in cahoots?"

Ariadne nodded. "Those boxes were my ticket out."

"You were going to steal my snuff boxes?" Jeramy cried, half-rising from his chair.

"They belonged to the one who found them," she replied with a defiant tilt to her chin. "By the by, your ex-partner fairly tore my husband's study apart looking for the one you had found, but it wasn't there. I still don't know where it is."

"Is it possible that someone saw you as you were hiding this Philip person away?" Abigail asked.

Ariadne ignored Abigail to glare defiantly at Jeramy as he settled himself in his chair. "Your partner needed no urging from me to smack that stevedore on the head and put chains to his feet." Returning her gaze to Abigail, she said, "You were asking too many questions, Miss Danforth. Getting too close to the truth. I would not kill anybody just to inherit her maid."

"But he had no hand in poisoning your husband, did he?" Abigail asked.

Ariadne shook her head. "After what Malcolm Tibault has done to me, if he were still alive, I would kill him again. Only this time I would make it a smaller dose so he would not die so fast."

"There, there, Mrs. Tibault," Amos said, casting an admiring glance at Abigail. "What you need is a sedative, and a nice long sleep." With a supportive arm around her shoulders, he helped her to her feet.

As Abigail and Maude stood, so did Peter and Jeramy.

"I say, Miss Danforth." Peter drew close to her. "You have cleared my name. How can I ever repay you?"

"You owe me nothing," she replied impatiently, recalling with no little guilt the thicket of social mores she was engaged in thinking about when she had wished to have a crime to solve.

"But have we not just saved each other's lives? Surely that must portend . . . something?" He suddenly found Abigail's ladylike modesty and demure demeanor quite irresistible, and a subtle but unmistakable shift took place in the nature of his interest in her. "I know I am rushing things, considering all that has happened, but I wonder if I might be permitted to call upon you when we reach New Orleans?" He glanced at Maude as if to seek her approval.

"I fear that would be quite impossible, Mr. Tibault," Abigail replied. "Our stay in the Crescent City will be brief, and our itinerary is booked to the full, I regret to say."

Maude took note of Peter's change in demeanor. With Ariadne no longer a rival, he was a rich and eminently suitable suitor. "Oh, but we could change—"

Before she could finish the sentence, Abigail used the unsteady motion of the ship as an excuse to appear to adjust her balance slightly and, swaying toward Maude, stepped firmly on her toe.

Maude winced. Knowing full well that Abigail's misstep had been deliberate, she quelled her protest for the moment, and allowed the crestfallen Peter to make his hasty excuses, and depart with Jeramy. But she could no longer remain silent when she and Abigail were finally settled side by side on their chaises, watching the rapid approach of landfall.

"Why were you so rude to Mr. Tibault when he sought to call upon you?" Maude said casually, masking her concern by following the flight of gulls circling above to greet the ship. "If you keep that up you will surely be an old maid."

Abigail considered her manners above reproach and was insulted by Maude's criticism. "I was not rude in the least," she replied defensively. Although she was loath to begin the familiar argument yet again, neither was she willing to back down.

"Your rejection was downright unseemly in its abruptness," Maude insisted, still gazing at the birds.

"Why can you not see that it is much kinder to turn him down now than allow him to get his hopes up that something might grow between us?" Abigail asked, genuinely puzzled that Maude could not see her side.

"How can you be so certain you could not learn to care for him?" Maude asked, equally puzzled.

Abigail shrugged. "He killed a man for one thing."

"But he was protecting you."

"I would have much preferred that he controlled his temper," Abigail said firmly.

"You must admit you do seem to have a predilection for courting danger, Miss Danforth." Maude did her best to sound as if she were stating a simple truth and not being accusatory. "It would seem to me that a protector might come in handy." She hesitated for a moment before adding with a slight shrug, "And he is most awfully rich."

"Humpff!" Abigail raked Maude with a fierce glance. "He has more money than is good for him, if you ask me. For lack of any interests of his own, he would no doubt soon be interfering with my investigations."

"That might not be an altogether bad thing, you know."

"Or demand that I have babies."

"What is the harm in that, pray?" Maude said. "Surely, someday, you will retire and raise a family."

"That is so improbable as to be impossible," Abigail said heatedly. "Just because I am of the female gender does not mean that marriage and babies must be my destiny."

"Can you not see that your quest for adventure is no different from Mr. Singleton's search for sunken treasure?" Maude asked with a reproving frown.

"I am willing to concede that Mr. Houdini made his point about illusion." Abigail shrugged nonchalantly, not displeased with Maude's assessment.

Surprised that Abigail had not taken umbrage at her remark, Maude cast a worried glance at the young detective. "Do you mean to say you never expect to fall in love?"

"I should think that even you would know better by now, Miss Cunningham." Abigail's eyes grew dark. "Or did you not notice that love is the greatest illusion of them all?"